A Tiger
Too Many

Antony Wootten

Eskdale Publishing
www.eskdale.150m.com

Eskdale Publishing , UK

First published in Great Britain in 2011 by Eskdale Publishing,
North Yorkshire

www.eskdale.150m.com

A Catalogue record for this book is available from the British
Library.

ISBN: 978-0-9537123-1-1

**Printed and bound in the UK by the MPG Books Group,
Bodmin and King's Lynn**

I would like to thank the late Clinton Keeling, the zoological historian who became my unofficial advisor while I was writing this novel. Clinton's detailed memories of London zoo, as well as events in the wider world during the war, which he willingly and patiently shared with me, were valuable beyond words.

Chapter 1

Adults tried not to show us they were scared about the war. But we already had our gas masks, and we'd helped with the preparations, like putting up the blackout curtains, and sticking tape across the windows to stop glass flying around if a bomb landed nearby. How could we not be scared? We just had to carry on as normal though. The war started on the 3rd of September 1939, and for me, everything changed the very next day. Even though it would be almost a year before the Germans came, that was the day the killing started.

Pete, my brother, was much older than me. He was a grown-up, and sometimes people thought he was my dad. But my dad had died when I was a baby. Pete worked in London Zoo, and whenever I could, I went with him to help. It was a Monday, but my school, and most public places, were closed, in case of bombing raids. The zoo was closed too, but only to the public. There was still lots of work to be done there. Mum was a housemaid for a rich lady in town, and she had to go to work as normal, so she said I had to go with Pete. I'd be safer there than on my own at home. It was sunny, but I had a dreadful sick feeling in my stomach. I could see the silvery barrage balloons in the sky. I liked the way they stayed up there, like kites, swaying peacefully, and changing shape very slightly in the wind. But I knew they were supposed to stop the Germans flying their planes low over London to drop bombs, and that made me feel afraid.

Pete was Junior Keeper in the Lion House. Mr Florey was in charge of the Lion House, but today he'd gone up to Whipsnade. The Lion House was a long, brick building. Outside, there were enclosures where some of the animals could walk about, but lots of animals were kept inside too. It wasn't just lions in the Lion House. There were Jaguars, tigers, and cheetahs. There were even two giant pandas, Tang and Ming. They were so soft and friendly looking, I loved watching them. I loved all the animals. But my favourite was Ronny, the oldest tiger. His orange stripes were the same colour as my hair. I thought he looked wise and gentle, and I felt sorry for him because he was getting old and was often ill.

But today, something was happening in the Reptile House. I could see it from outside Ronny's cage. It was at the other end of Broad Walk, the wide path which ran through the middle of the zoo. I'd seen the keepers coming and going with boxes, and the man in the suit with his clipboard, and the lorry parked outside. I followed Pete round for ages, getting in his way, asking him what they were doing. Eventually, when we were having a break in the keepers' room upstairs, he told me.

And I couldn't believe it.

"Why do they have to *kill* them?" I gasped.

"Jill, Sugar," Pete said softly, putting his big hand on my shoulder. Pete always called me Sugar. He called other people 'Honey'; well, girls and ladies anyway. But 'Sugar' was just for me. "I know how you feel," he said, stooping so his blue eyes were right in front of me. "But, you know, there's a war on now, the zoo could get bombed. If any of those snakes got out, it would be really dangerous. If one of them bit someone... Some of them can kill, you know."

I knew Pete was right, and I'd been coming here with him for long enough to know that sometimes animals had to be killed if they were sick or injured. But killing healthy animals seemed so unfair. They couldn't help being poisonous. The lump in my throat wouldn't go away, even when Pete hugged me. He stroked one of my plaits. "I wouldn't have brought you today if I'd known. No-one tells me anything. Anyway, it's not all bad. I've got a surprise for you a bit later. You'll love it. I promise." He squeezed my cheek. Pete knew I hated it when other people did that, and he only did it as a joke. Usually I'd laugh, and then maybe punch him in the arm. But today I just turned, and went outside.

"Don't do anything that'll get me the sack!" Pete called.

I didn't want to help Pete today. Today I just wanted to wander around, looking at the animals, and trying to forget the poor snakes and the war. I had my heavy gas mask hanging at my side. The string was already digging into my shoulder, but Mum said I had to carry it wherever I went, now.

I could smell a bonfire somewhere. The zoo was almost deserted, and Ronny was pacing backwards and forwards in his enclosure. I leaned on the barrier and watched him through the thick wire mesh. He always had his head down these days. He seemed sad, and tired. Pete said the enclosures never got any sun, and the cold North Wind could blow right into them. That's not good for a tiger. I wished I could save him, take him somewhere warm to live. He looked at me. I loved it when he did that. Some of the other animals never looked at you, as if they couldn't even see the people outside their cages. But Ronny always looked at the visitors. Sometimes he growled at them, or jumped at the side of his enclosure, making it shake and rattle, and the people scream. I gazed back at Ronny's dark eyes. I knew he was only teasing.

I could hear the howler monkey whooping now, and the chattering of the birds in the nearby Bird House. But when the zoo was closed like this, it always surprised me how quiet the animals really were.

Opposite Ronny's enclosure were the wolves. They paced up and down all the time, and the wind ruffled the fluffy hair on their backs. I watched them for a while, then wandered up onto Broad Walk. I was going towards the big pond, to see the penguins, when I heard a gunshot. I recognised it straight away. That's how they killed the bigger animals. Surely not snakes though. Pete hadn't said any of the bigger animals were being killed today.

There was another gunshot. It was close by. I suddenly wondered if maybe it wasn't the zoo-people at all. I froze in terror. Had the Germans come here already? But why would the Germans come and attack the zoo? No, animals were being killed. With my gas mask box banging against my side, I ran back past the wolves, towards the Antelope House. I was sure the noise had come from there.

I could already see the zoo lorry parked outside the front. Six men came out of the building, carrying a large animal in a sort of canvass hammock. It was like a big deer, with a ruddy-brown back and stripes on its legs. An eland. They swung it up onto the back of the lorry, making it bounce as the animal landed. They pulled the hammock out, and went back inside with it. A few minutes later they came back out again. This time they had a smaller animal, with short horns. It was a zebu. Soon it was on the lorry beside the eland, its legs sticking up in the air at an angle, like dead trees, and the men were mopping their brows.

I couldn't understand it. I knew about the snakes, but these two animals were so gentle. They wouldn't hurt anyone even if they did get out. Why did they have to die?

A man in a suit came out next. He was holding a clipboard. He had an old-fashioned bowler hat on and his gas mask box strung across his body. I wiped my eyes, took a deep breath and walked right up to him.

"Excuse me," I said, all calm, like my mum when she gets cross with someone. "Please kindly tell me why you are having these animals shot." I had my hands on my hips.

He looked down at me. "Hello, young lady," he said. "Pete Larch's little sister isn't it?" I nodded. He sighed, and looked around at the other men. They all just looked away and started talking.

I carried on looking up at him, trying to be stern.

He crouched down in front of me and smiled. "My, you're a bold one, eh?" he said, and squeezed my cheek. I just looked back at him, without reacting. He stopped smiling. He sighed again, and said, "My dear, sometimes, so others can go on living, some have to be... sacrificed."

"Why?" I said.

"It's... complicated."

"But... they're not even dangerous like the snakes."

"No."

"Were they ill then?"

"Er... They were old and... they needed a lot of medicine. It's... it's a lot to do with money. It's very complicated." He cleared his throat.

But suddenly I had a horrible thought. "Are you going to kill all the dangerous or old animals?"

"Not all of them, no. Of course not." He smiled again.

"What about the tigers?"

"Well..." He stood up and looked around at the others. He waved one of them over, and whispered something to him. I heard what he said. He'd sent for Pete. The other man hurried off. I could feel tears pricking at my eyes. I shook my head. I couldn't speak. I walked away slowly. "Come back," the man in the suit said. I didn't, so he tried again, more firmly this time, like a teacher. But I kept walking.

I was about to break into a run when I saw Pete coming towards us. He must have already been on his way to find me. "Pete," I shouted as I ran up to him. He hugged me, lifting me up.

"What's wrong, Sugar?"

"It's Ronny. They're going to kill him."

I'd expected Pete to be horrified. But he just lowered me to the ground and held my hands. "I know. I've just found out."

"Well..." I began. "Well... aren't you going to stop them?"

"I wish I could. I wish I could. But it's for the

best."

I didn't know what to say. For a moment, I just stared at him with my mouth wide open. How could he just let this happen? I hated him suddenly.

But if he wasn't going to do anything, I'd have to.

I looked around at the other men, who seemed to be watching me as if I was one of their dangerous animals and needed to be captured. The man in the suit gave me kindly smile, but it didn't work. I ran again. This time I knew where to run to. I'd only ever heard of Doctor Barker, the man in charge of the whole zoo. I didn't really know what he looked like, but I knew his office must be in the big building on the other side of the zoo. Somehow, I would stop the killing. I would save Ronny.

Chapter 2

I held my gas mask box still as I ran. Past the Camel House. Across the big courtyard, past the main restaurant and the Tea Pavilion. My chest and legs were sore now. I got faster where the path sloped down towards the tunnel under the road. The offices were on the other side. I was nearly out of control. My feet hurt from the hard cobble stones and my steps echoed as I sped through the tunnel. I could hardly breathe now but I wouldn't stop. Another lorry at the end of the tunnel. Men unloading sand-bags there. I darted between them. Some of them called after me.

The path sloped up, away from the tunnel, making my legs ache even more. I was on the other side of the road now. Past the Insect House, and there was the office building. I heaved the door open, and went inside. There was an old lady behind a desk. She asked where I was going and I told her, as calmly as I could, I needed to see Doctor Barker. She shook her head and said something about a meeting, but I ran past her and up the wide staircase. I was on a landing now, which smelt of polish and old carpet. There were doors on either side, with names on. I was panting for breath and I could hear the lady coming up the stairs behind me.

I carried on along the landing, slowly though, so I could read the names on the office doors at the same time. My face was sweaty and burning hot. I didn't want to meet Doctor Barker like this, but I had no choice.

Suddenly, a door in front of me opened, and I ran straight into the big man who stepped out. He grabbed onto me and managed to stop us both from falling over.

"Young lady," snapped the man. Then, the woman chasing me, sounding all out of breath, said, "Doctor Barker, I do apologise for this."

"Doctor Barker?" I said. I couldn't believe my luck. My heart was beating fast from my run, but I was excited now too. I had found him. I would make him listen. I would save Ronny!

I looked up at him. He was fat and tall. He had white hair and spectacles and was wearing a black, pin-striped suit. He looked very confused and a little bit cross.

"Yes. And who might you be, young lady?"

The woman was beside me now. She was red-faced from running. "So sorry, Doctor Barker," she said. "I tried to stop her, but she just ran past. She said she needed to see you, but I told her you were—"

"It's quite all right," he said sharply. He looked down at me. His face was stern. "Who are you?"

I quickly told him I was Pete's sister, but I didn't mention Ronny yet.

"And you were looking for me?"

"Yes," I said.

"Well, come on child, spit it out. What do you want?"

"They're going to shoot Ronny!" I said, still trying to get my breath back.

"Ronny?"

"The tiger. Ronny the tiger! They're going to shoot him!" I couldn't think what else to say.

He looked confused for a moment, but then he said, "Ah yes, and about time too. The poor creature's been a drain on our finances for years. Now, run along. This is no place for a child."

"What? No, no, they're going to *kill* him. Don't you understand?"

The lady started trying to pry me away from Doctor Barker now. She spoke softly to me, but I ignored her.

"You can't let them do it!" I gasped. "It's not

fair!"

"Sadly, my dear, life is not fair," Doctor Barker said. "That is a lesson you had better get learned, and fast. There's a war on now, you know. Things are likely to get a darned sight more unfair. If you came running up here every time I gave the order to kill one of the animals, you'd soon wear out my carpet. And if I listened to you, and withdrew my order, the whole place would be overrun with sick, weak, infirm and elderly creatures who would no more wish to be here on this Earth than the public would wish to see them. The place would be a shambles and a disaster. A forest cannot thrive without a good fire every once in a while, did you know that?"

I shook my head. My mouth was open wide.

"Well now you do. Good day to you. Would someone please escort this young lady back to wherever she came from?"

With that, he strode off down the corridor.

I was helpless. I heard a couple of distant bangs. I wasn't sure if they were gunfire. I felt sick and exhausted. And *angry*. I couldn't believe what had just happened. Was I dreaming? Had Doctor Barker really said all that about Ronny?

"He's a lovely old tiger," the lady said. "I am

sorry. Come on, I'll take you over. We'll find your brother."

***

We walked back to the Lion House. I didn't run. I knew I couldn't save Ronny now. If I ran, I'd only get there in time to see him getting shot. We'd heard a few gunshots already. As we came up the slope from the tunnel, I let the bright, painful sunlight burn into my eyes.

It seemed to take forever. We passed the camels who were just standing there as if nothing was wrong. They didn't know about the war and they didn't know about the killing.

I could see from a distance the lorry was already outside the Lion House. I stopped. I felt really sick.

"Maybe you should wait here," the lady said. "I'll go and get your brother over."

I couldn't speak, but I shook my head and started walking again. My eyes stung. I didn't want to wipe them because I didn't want the lady to know I was crying, but after a while I could hardly see. I just let her lead me by the hand. Eventually, I had to blink. Big tears fell and my eyes cleared. Pete was standing outside the Lion

House with his head down. He must have known I wouldn't want to look at him. I could see that same group of men with sweaty faces, and the man in his bowler hat and suit, writing on a clip board. Mr Florey, the Lion House head-keeper, was there too now.

Ronny was lying on the lorry, next to the Zebu and Eland. His tongue was hanging out.

I let go of the lady's hand. Pete came over to me, but I walked past him, and all the others. I stood beside the lorry and looked up at Ronny's dark eyes. I reached up and stroked his leg. His fur was soft and warm. He smelt of wet grass. I'd never touched him before. He'd have eaten me of course, but still, I wished I could have touched him when he was alive. Then I turned away. I walked back past everyone, and into the Lion House. I went upstairs, to the keeper's room, and sat down on the old wooden bench.

Pete came up the stairs just as the lorry's engine started. He stood in the doorway for a moment, as if he was nervous of me. Then he came and knelt in front of me.

"I'm so sorry," he said. Suddenly I realised he'd been crying too. That was when I knew there was nothing he could have done to save Ronny. "He was old, Sugar, and he wasn't well," he said. "It was nothing to do with the war." I didn't want to hate him, so I let him hug me. Pete was right. I knew Ronny had been sick for ages, and was very old, and probably wasn't happy any more. I always loved him more than the other animals because of it. I knew zoo animals were usually killed when they got like that though. I just hated it. "He's in a better place now," Pete said softly. "He isn't limping anymore you know. I'll bet you he's happier than ever." It seemed like ages before he let go of me.

Mr Florey had come up the stairs by now. He smiled at me, but it was a sad smile, not like his usual one. He was round, jolly man, and his black hair was starting to go silver at the sides. He had spectacles and a moustache, and whenever I saw him he was wearing his old blue boiler suit and Wellington boots. I wiped my eyes and tried to stop sniffing.

"Hello, Jill," he said, and sat at the large desk. There was nothing much else in the room, just a tall wooden wardrobe for coats, a tiny sink in one corner and a black stove with a kettle on top in another. "It's been a tough day, mm?" I nodded. "If I'd known they were going to do that today, dear, I would have insisted Pete didn't bring you. It's not nice to see something like that. We're all going to miss him, you know. I loved him myself. There were quite a few damp eyes out there, I can tell you. Grown men an' all, and I count myself among them." I sniffed, and tried to smile. "Well now, Pete," Mr Florey said, opening the big ledger book he always wrote in, and dipping the pen in the ink well. "Have you shown Jill what I brought from Whipsnade?"

Pete shook his head. "I want you to see something," Pete said to me. "It'll make you feel better."

How could anything make me feel better after what had happened? Pete turned and went back downstairs. Wiping my nose on my sleeve, I followed him. I couldn't imagine what he was going to show me, and it felt wrong for me to be interested in something else at a time like this. But I was. I couldn't help it.

Downstairs was a wide passageway called the service corridor behind all the animal enclosures, the inside animals on one side and the outside animals on the other. There were some big cupboards, and an enormous refrigerator which all the meat was kept in for the animals to eat. There were windows into the enclosures, but the only two outside windows in the service corridor were in the doors at each end. Like all windows, they had tape across them, and there were blackout curtains too, but they were open. Still, the corridor seemed darker than ever.

Pete opened the door to one of the empty indoor enclosures, but I didn't follow him.

"Come on, Sugar," he said.

I shook my head. "I don't want to." I tried to see round him anyway, but it was too dark.

Pete closed the door again.

"Why not?"

I just looked at the floor.

"Ronny won't mind, you know. He won't think it means you're not sad about him, or that you've forgotten him." He stroked one of my plaits again. I nodded. He opened the door and I followed him inside. I couldn't help it, I was curious. We were standing in the dark sleeping-space. It had a tiny window, so you could see in from the service corridor, and a low opening at the other end that led out into the larger enclosure.

I couldn't see much at first because it was dark. Then I saw a wooden crate on the floor, with its front off. There was straw all over the place.

"I told you I'd have a surprise for you," Pete said.

I still couldn't see what it was. I crouched down. I could smell that tiger-smell of grass and warmth and straw. There was a tiny bundle of fur in there. I could barely make it out, but I'd already guessed what it was.

"He's from Whipsnade Park Zoo. His mother rejected him," Pete said. "It happens sometimes. He's the runt, and he's sick, so she doesn't want him." After everything that had happened today, I wanted to hate Pete's surprise. But I couldn't, of course. Nobody could. "They sent him here because our infirmary's got better facilities for looking after him. Mr Florey brought him down. Got here while you were out there causing trouble." It didn't make sense. I thought today was a day for getting rid of animals, not getting new ones. "Reckon Mr Florey and I will need some help looking after him. Can you think of anyone who'd be up for the job?" I didn't want to smile, but in the end I couldn't help it. I hoped Ronny would forgive me.

The little tiger cub was sleeping all on his own. I stroked his soft fur with the back of my fingers, gently, so I wouldn't wake him. I could feel his warmth.

"Is he going to get better?" I said.

"Mr Florey says they think so. He's going to need medicine though. Runts often do. And a bit of extra love won't do him any harm either." He grinned. "If they thought he was a lost cause, they'd have..." I knew what they'd have done. Pete didn't need to say it. "He's going to wake up for a feed soon," Pete said. "I'd better go and prepare his bottle."

Chapter 3

I loved him straight away. He was so small, bigger than a kitten though, about the size of a puppy. He was heavy too, and floppy. Mr Florey said I could be the one to name him, so I called him Ronny the Second, but we didn't always say the 'Second' bit, so really it was just Ronny. He walked as if he was half asleep, staggering a little, and bumping against things a lot. I was usually allowed to go into his enclosure, and when I pulled him onto my lap, he lay there, breathing softly. He even purred! That surprised me. I don't know why, but I hadn't expected tigers to purr. His purr was like a little, contented growl. He was so soft and warm, and his eyes were dark brown, like Ronny the First's.

But even so, I had a sick feeling in my stomach the whole time. People had been building air-raid shelters wherever they could. There were ten in the zoo, including the tunnels under the road which had been partly blocked with sandbags at both ends. One had been built in our school playground long before the war started, so we all knew the Germans were going to come and drop bombs on us. People built air-raid shelters in their gardens,

21

but we lived in a first floor flat in Princess Terrace, and we didn't have a garden. So we had a Morrison shelter, which was like a cage under the kitchen table. In fact, the whole table was made of metal. It felt cold all the time, even through the table cloth. The worst thing about it was that you couldn't sit at the table properly anymore. The cage stopped you being able to put your legs under. You were supposed to take the sides off when you were using it as a table, but we didn't.

Ronny the Second wasn't scared of the war though. I suppose he didn't even know there was one. He was always so happy. He loved playing, jumping about and chasing my hand, or the end of a bit of straw. School was open again now, but lots of children had been evacuated to the countryside, where they'd be safe away from the German bombs. Some of my best friends had gone. I missed them, but as soon as the bell went at the end of the day, I would head up to the zoo as fast as I could. It wasn't far. Our flat was only a few yards away from the school gate, and the zoo was just a few minutes from there. Mum was always still at work, so she didn't mind me going up to the zoo, as long as I told her beforehand. She said she was happier knowing I was with Pete, rather than alone at home. I always ran. Up Princess Terrace, past the pub where Pete often met his friends, across the road and past the old stone church, then I'd stop and watch for cars before crossing Prince Albert Road. The heavy cardboard box with my gas mask in banged against my leg all the time, and the string dug into my shoulder, but I didn't care.

The zoo was at one end of Regent's Park. If you were walking in the park you could see some of the animals over the walls, and through the fences. But the zoo's front entrance was right there on Prince Albert Road. While the zoo was still closed to the public, Pete would wait for me and let me in the staff gate. Sometimes he was late, or wasn't there, but there was usually someone else around. If it was Pete, we'd walk the rest of the way, and chat. But if I was alone, I'd start running again, round the corner and over the bridge that crossed the canal. The boats below were full of coal, and their steam engines made blue smoke, just like trains. It was strange that the canal went right through the zoo, but at least it meant that the men on the barges could get a little peek at some of the animals as they chugged on through. Then, I'd pass the offices where Doctor Barker worked. I wouldn't even look at them in case he was there. The rest of my journey always reminded me of that horrible day. I hoped Ronny the First knew how much I missed him.

Mr Florey always let me give Ronny the Second his evening feed. I held the little tiger cub on my lap, tummy-up. I loved his warmth and his smell. Some days, he didn't seem to want his milk, but when he did, he would go all still in my lap as I placed the bottle in his mouth. He'd make little squelching noises as he sucked at it, and he even sometimes burped. When he'd finished, he would either creep slowly back into his crate, or stay lying there, on me. I would rock him to sleep as if he really was my baby.

But one day, as I went along the corridor in the Lion House, I heard voices coming from Ronny's enclosure. One was Mr Florey's, and the other... I pushed open the door. I saw Doctor Barker standing there, with his hands on his hips, looking down at Ronny. Ronny was curled up in the straw, sleeping. Doctor Barker raised his eyebrows when he saw me coming in. Pete was standing beside Mr Florey, with his hands in his pockets. He smiled at me, but I could tell something was wrong.

"Ah, young lady," Doctor Barker said. "We meet again." He talked too loud, and I thought he might wake Ronny. "I hear you've taken a shine to this little feller."

"She's been quite an asset," Mr Florey said. He looked worried, and I could tell he wanted me to go.

"Well, young lady. Keen on animals are you?" I nodded. "Jolly good. However, if you do want to keep coming here, there are some home truths you need to learn. I can't have you causing trouble every time you see something you don't like."

"Oh, Jill's no trouble," Mr Florey said.

Ronny stirred, and stretched his front legs.

Doctor Barker bent down and put his hand on my shoulder. He removed his spectacles, and I saw his eyes were smaller than I thought. "This tiger is sick, young lady. That is why his mother rejected him. Sometimes he doesn't take his milk for days, and when he does he often doesn't keep it down." I felt cold with fear, but I knew what he was saying was true. I'd just never thought it was anything to worry about. I knew babies were often sick, and some animals too. It wasn't always something serious. But Doctor Barker sounded very serious. "He needs medicine every day, and that medicine costs money. Money that could be spent on feeding and breeding healthy animals. I'm afraid if he doesn't start showing an improvement soon, he will be K.B.O. That means killed by order. My order. There are too many other wonderful creatures in this zoo for me to waste money on a lost cause. Especially now there's a war on. If you want to come to my zoo, and spend time with my tiger, you must be strong enough to accept the fact that it is for the best." My legs felt weak. I could not believe what he had just said, and I certainly would never accept it. "Can you do that?" he said. I had no choice. I felt as if I was betraying Ronny, but I nodded, and hoped my tears didn't show. "Good," he said, and put his spectacles back on. "Three times a day, Mr Florey," he said, and Mr Florey nodded. Then Doctor Barker left. I listened to his shoes on the concrete, and then the outside door opened and closed.

"Jill, Sugar," Pete said, and stroked my arm.

Mr Florey smiled at me, but I couldn't smile back. I knelt down next to Ronny. He looked so peaceful and happy. I stroked his paw and he stretched out his toes.

"Sorry you had to hear it like that," Mr Florey said. "I should have told you myself."

"Yer, so should I," Pete said. "I just hoped it was nothing too serious."

I couldn't reply.

Chapter 3

And now the war wasn't the only thing I felt sick about.

Chapter 4

I thought about Ronny all the time. My mind was full of him. I even saw his little face when I was trying to sleep at night. I worried myself sick about him, after what Doctor Barker had said. But, after a few weeks, we could see he was getting bigger and much stronger. Everyone seemed pleased with the way he was growing. I was sure he was getting better.

It was a Saturday, and I had persuaded Mum to come to the zoo. She'd said she was really busy. But I'd begged and pleaded with her, and she'd finally agreed. I really wanted her to meet Ronny. Mum brushed my hair for me, and made me wear my best dress. She put on hers too. It was light blue with little green and red flowers all over it. Sometimes, after a long day at work, she looked old and tired, but that day, I thought she looked beautiful, with her hair down, and her red lipstick on. She'd made me polish my shoes. They were pretty dirty before, but they were shiny again now. Mum had smart shoes with a little bow and a bit of a heel, and she wore a tiny hat. I could smell her perfume. She even let me dab a bit on my neck, as if I was a grown up.

The zoo was open to the public again now, and you would hardly have known there was a war on. Everything seemed the same as before, except for the brown boxes people had at their sides. The camels, llamas, elephants and Shetland ponies were all giving their rides up and down Elephant Walk, and people crowded round to watch the feeding times in the animal houses. The polar bear was always popular. So was the chimpanzee's tea party. No-one looked as if they were worried about the war.

Even though many children had been evacuated to the countryside, there still seemed to be as many as ever in the zoo with their mums and dads. Seeing them made me wonder about my dad. He died when I was a baby, so I never even really knew him. But I'd seen grey photos of him, and Mum and Pete told me he was tall and strong, and funny too. He'd have carried me on his shoulders, telling me stories and taking me to interesting places. If my dad was alive, Mum wouldn't have to work, so she wouldn't always be so tired, and we'd have family picnics in the park, or days out in the country side. Maybe we'd even have a car.

Somehow, I imagined Dad would know how to

make things better. Even Ronny.

I felt proud that day though, walking along the cobbled paths with my mum, looking at the animals together.

She didn't want to come too close to Ronny at first. She was a bit scared, I think. Mum liked animals, but she didn't love them the way Pete and I did. She didn't sit on the floor like me because it was all covered in straw, but she did crouch down next to me.

"Phoo," she said, smiling, and waving her hand in front of her nose. I laughed. It did smell quite bad in Ronny's enclosure, but I hardly ever noticed that. Then she started to stroke Ronny's fur, just behind his ear. She got it right first time: that's where Ronny liked it best.

The door opened, and Pete came in. Mr Florey was behind him, and there was another man with him. He had thick yellow hair in a parting, and he had one of those curly moustaches. He was tall, and dressed in country tweed, with long, woolly socks. His trousers were the ones that stop half way down, and button up just under the knees. He was smoking a pipe, which he handed to Mr Florey, as if Mr Florey was his servant. He was also wearing a monocle, and when he saw me sitting there with Ronny on my lap, he let it fall, and hang on its chord.

"So beautiful," he said softly. And he smiled at my mum. She stood up and dusted herself down, even though she wasn't dirty.

Mr Florey said, "Mrs Larch, this is Mr Fred Kendal. He's a friend of the zoo, and has quite an animal collection of his own in Kent."

Mum and Mr Kendal shook hands. "Do call me Fred," he said.

"Joanna," my mum said, and it seemed like ages before Mr Kendal let go of her hand.

"You must be Jill," Mr Kendal said then, and crouched down next to me. I could see he was younger than I'd first though, but his moustache and monocle had made him seem much older. I nodded. He smelt funny. Not just his breath: that smelt of his pipe smoke. There was another, strange smell. It was sweet, and sharp. I recognised it but couldn't think what it was. Pete made a disgusted face at me, and pinched his nose. I tried not to laugh. Mum didn't notice. Mr Kendal was gazing at Ronny now.

"Oh for a tiger," he said, stroking him on the back. "I have many of God's fabulous and wonderful creatures in my menagerie, but I don't have a tiger." Even though he used big words, he didn't sound posh like I expected. "Poor thing," he said, and sighed.

"Poor thing?" I said.

"Well, not doing too well, is he. Not growing the way he should." My heart did a flip. Even though Mr Kendal hadn't told me anything I didn't already know, I hated hearing him say it.

"Oh, ah," Mr Florey interrupted him. "I think he'll be fine, Mr Kendal."

Pete said, "Let's leave Ronny to sleep." As they all shuffled out, Mum crouched down next to me again.

"Sorry love," she said, stroking my hair. She kissed me on the cheek. I couldn't look at her. Tears were burning my eyes. I looked down at Ronny. He was sleeping now. I always thought he seemed strong and healthy these days, but I did know he still sometimes didn't eat or drink anything all day. He slept a lot too. I wished he could just get well.

My mum wiped my face with her handkerchief. "He's very lucky, you know, to have someone like you loving him so much."

I smiled, but really I felt sick now. I kissed Ronny's fur. I whispered, "I'll always be here." He made a tiny grunting noise, as if he understood.

Pete came back in then. "Mr Kendal's going to get in with his wolves," he said.

"Get *in* with them?" Mum replied.

"Yes, he's got a couple of wolves that're kept here. He likes to get in with them! Come and see!"

"Isn't that dangerous?" Mum said.

"He'll be all right. He's covered himself with aniseed. They love the smell. Can't get enough of it." With that, Pete went.

"Well," Mum said. "I just hope they don't think he's one big aniseed ball and eat him up."

We both laughed.

That evening, over dinner, Pete couldn't stop talking about Mr Kendal. Mum said she thought he was an oaf, but I knew she only said that because he'd upset me. Pete said the wolves had clambered all over him, licking him as if they loved him. There were huge crowds of people watching; everyone was amazed.

And then a telegram arrived. I think Mum and Pete knew what it was straight away. They both went quiet. Mum thanked the telegram boy and closed the door. Pete stood up and she handed it to him. He didn't open it at first. I didn't understand. Was it going to be something bad? Mum sat back down at the table. She reached across and held my hand. I was really worried now. I looked up at Pete. He smiled, but his eyes weren't sparkling. He read the telegram, then passed it to Mum.

"What is it, Mum?" I asked

She squeezed my hand and I saw tears in her eyes.

"I'm going to join the war," Pete said. "I've been called up," and he fired an invisible gun.

Chapter 5

I suppose I was too young to know what war would be like for the soldiers. If I had, I would have been much more worried about Pete. I didn't want him to go, but that was because I wanted him to be near me all the time. I didn't really think about, or *know* about the danger for Pete. Lots of people were saying the war would be over by Christmas anyway. There still hadn't been any air-raids, and some people were calling it a phony war. We were all starting to relax a bit. Lots of the children who had been evacuated had even started to come back.

But Pete did go. I remember saying goodbye to him at the station. The big train was hissing like an angry camel. It was making little whistling noises and filling the crowded station with smoke and steam. Pete looked tall and proud. He was wearing his long woollen coat, he'd brushed his hair, and his shoes were shiny. He hugged me and kissed my head. I couldn't help crying. I didn't want to let go of him. "Don't worry about me, Sugar," Pete said. "I'll be home in a couple of months. I'll write." There were hundreds of other men Pete's age getting on the train, and they all looked happy and excited. Pete knew some of them. He'd been in their class at school. There were lots of mums and dads and little brothers and sisters saying goodbye to them all. The guard shouted that the train was about to leave.

Pete kissed Mum, and she hugged him for so long I thought he was going to miss the train. Then, he picked up his trunk and climbed aboard. The guard blew the whistle and the train creaked and clanked and started to move. Pete leaned out of the window, waving as the train slowly pulled out of the station. Eventually, the steam and smoke wrapped round him like fog. It was really sad to watch him go, but it didn't occur to me that I might never see him again.

I still went to the zoo every day after school, even though it was getting darker sooner and was quite cold too. Mr Florey said I was his helper now. They knew me at the gate and let me in free. Ronny seemed to be getting bigger and stronger every day. I wished Pete could be with me to see him grow.

All through autumn, no bombs fell on us.

Pete wrote to us every two weeks or so. He was in France. The Germans hadn't arrived yet. He seemed to be his usual happy and jolly self. He said he'd made a lot of friends. He always said how much he missed us, and how terrible the army food was. Sometimes, though, some of the ladies in villages they were camping in would take dinner to the soldiers, or invite some of them in for Sunday roast. He said it didn't matter that they didn't speak the same language. They still managed to get along.

Pete always asked about Ronny. When I wrote my letters back to him, I told him all about how Ronny liked to play and climb on me, even though he was already getting to be too big for that. I also told him about the changes at the zoo, like the ponies and llamas being used to pull carts because of the petrol shortage. I told him how Ronny had started eating proper meat, and didn't need the milk and special meals any more. And I told him Doctor Barker had reduced the dosage of Ronny's medicine. I was excited about that. He was getting better. He was going to be all right!

It was an incredibly cold winter. Mum and I cooked together, preparing for Christmas. In November, Mum had to register at our local shop because soon some foods were going to be rationed, which meant we'd only be able to have a little bit of them every week. But we were still going to try and have a really big feast at Christmas, first. We needed it too, it was so cold.

I'll never forget Christmas eve. It was getting dark, and I was freezing when I walked home from the zoo. It was hard to be excited about Christmas, since Pete would not be there to enjoy it with us, but being with Ronny always cheered me up, especially now that he seemed stronger and healthier than ever before. He made me forget the war, too. But outside, even though it was only about six o'clock, the blackout made the streets dimmer and gloomier than usual. It was quiet too, because most people stayed indoors. An A.R.P. officer, the person who made sure everyone was keeping their blackout curtains closed and taking care to prevent air-raids, smiled at me. "Merry Christmas," he said, and raised his tin hat.

"Merry Christmas," I replied, and smiled back. A car went by. Its lamps were half blacked out, which gave it a sad expression.

The kitchen was always the warmest room in the flat because of the boiler which heated the water. It stood beside the electric cooker, and had a big silver chimney which went up through the roof. The chimney was always hot, and so were the water pipes behind it. Mum and I always sat close to it when we ate our breakfast, and sometimes our tea too. I was looking forward to warming my hands by the boiler's chimney. But when I opened the kitchen door I stopped. There was a man sitting at the table with Mum. He had his back to me but I could see he had really short, cropped hair, like a soldier. I put my satchel down and walked into the room, trying to see the stranger's face. He and Mum stopped talking, and Mum grinned at me as if she knew something exciting was about to happen.

And suddenly I couldn't believe my eyes. He must have heard me come in, but he pretended to be looking at his nails. I thought he wasn't even going to say hello to me.

I said, "Pete?" and he started laughing. He jumped up and grabbed hold of me, squeezing me tight. "Hello, Sugar," he said, and whirled me round. "Wow, it's good to be home," he said. And I knew right then that we were going to have a fantastic Christmas.

The flat was full of cooking smells. The turkey was on the kitchen table in a huge dish, all ready to be cooked tomorrow, and it was actually snowing outside now. Pete and I went down to the yard to fill the scuttles with coal and coke so we wouldn't have to go out again until tomorrow. Mum and I had put up holly above the windows and hung it on the walls. We'd made paper chains from newspaper too. We had a small tree in the sitting room window, and Pete got a fire roaring in the grate. Somehow, the blackout curtains made everything seem cosier.

We had carol singers knocking at our door that evening. They were a man and a woman and their three children. They looked freezing cold, so we invited them in and gave them mince pies and hot cocoa. We sang carols together around the cold, metal table. No matter how much heat the boiler gave off, the metal table always felt ice-cold. We had good fun though. Pete danced round the kitchen with the Lady whose name was Gladys. It made us all laugh. Before they left, we gave the family some money, and they said we were true friends.

I barely slept, and when I woke there was thick snow on the ground and still falling. Both my grans came round for dinner, bringing armfuls of presents. My grans were best friends. Granny Crow, my mum's mum, was tall and stern, but she had a soft voice and a kind smile. Granny Larch, my dad's mum, was short and round and rosy faced. She had a booming loud laugh and always said, "Don't mind if I do," whenever someone offered her an adult drink like wine or gin. Mum said they bickered together like an old married couple, but I never noticed, and we always had fun when they came round.

It seemed everyone had known Pete was coming home, but me. In fact, Mum had only found out a day or two ago. We'd already sent his presents out to him in the post. Mine was a little wooden tiger from the zoo shop. He hadn't received them yet, though.

After dinner, Pete got out some old gramophone records and we had another sing and a dance. You had to wind the gramophone up, and we laughed when the music got slower and slower as it wound down again. Later, Granny Larch played the piano. Our piano was out of tune and some of the keys didn't work, but that just made us laugh too. Granny Larch shrieked with laughter whenever she forgot the notes, and Granny Crow called her a noisy old crone, but we all knew she didn't mean it. All day long I wore the thick, woolly scarf Pete had bought me. He'd also bought me a teddy bear that looked like a tiger and I hugged it even as we danced.

The day after boxing day, I took Pete to see Ronny. They played together like best friends. "He's so strong!" Pete said afterwards. "You'd never know he was the runt of the litter." Then Ronny started sniffing at my gas mask box. It was getting really battered and old looking already, and was worn through at the corners. The rubber gas mask smelt a bit of fish. Maybe that's why Ronny was so interested in it. Normally I'd just move the box away from him, but Pete had a different idea. He took the gas mask out and showed it to Ronny. Ronny was all confused, and he went a bit strange, lying flat on the floor, with his bottom in the air. He made little growling noises as if he thought the gas mask must be some strange new animal. I started to laugh. Then Pete put it on, although it was really tight on him. Ronny backed away at first, and hid in the straw. Then he sneaked back out again, and slowly came up to Pete.

"Hello, Ronny," Pete said. The mask made his voice sound deep and distant. Ronny was startled, and backed away again.

I rubbed his side and said, "It's all right, Ronny. It's Pete. Don't tease him, Pete." Pete was laughing now. Then, Pete did what my friends and I always did when we were having air-raid practices in the shelter at school. He made a loud rasping noise by blowing hard into the mask so the air came out round the sides, between the rubber and his face. It always made the teachers cross, and it made Ronny bound into me, trying to get inside my coat. I think Ronny thought he was still a tiny cub, but actually he was like a medium sized dog now, heavy and strong, and he almost knocked me over backwards.

"Stop teasing him," I said crossly, even though I wanted to laugh. Pete pulled the mask off. His face was red and his eyes watering. He was laughing. He put the mask down and grabbed Ronny. He wrapped his long arms round Ronny's chest, and then rubbed him all over. "I'm sorry, old feller," he said, burying his face in Ronny's fur. "It's me, Pete!"

And Ronny seemed happy again.

A little later, Mr Florey came in to give Ronny his medicine. I always hated watching him tip Ronny's head back, and push the big, white, calcium tablet into the back of his throat. Ronny let him do it, even though his teeth were so big now I was sure he could have bitten Mr Florey's fingers off if he'd wanted to. Then Mr Florey stroked Ronny's throat until the tablet was gone. He even checked inside Ronny's mouth to make sure. Mr Florey must have had a special way with animals though because Ronny made his deep, throbbing purr, and seemed perfectly happy throughout the whole unpleasant process. After that, Mr Florey and Pete chatted for ages while I stroked Ronny. I didn't listen to their conversation, and when they made some excuse to step out into the corridor together, I knew it was because they didn't want me to hear them talking about Ronny's health. I just stared at my tiger, and thought how content he seemed, all warm and cosy in the straw. When Mr Florey had gone, Pete crouched down beside me and stroked Ronny's head.

"He's grown so much," Pete said. "He's looking really well."

I nodded. Then, I couldn't stop myself asking, "Is he?" Mr Florey was always kind to me, but I knew he didn't tell me everything, and I knew the tablets meant Ronny was still not well.

Pete sighed, and we watched Ronny sleep. "He's definitely getting stronger," Pete said at last. "He is still small for his age though. You know that, don't you? But he's getting better. His immune system's getting stronger, so he'll be able to fight infections off and stay healthy if we keep on looking after him like this. And you make him so happy. You make his life special. That's all that matters." I nodded. I just wished I could feel as happy as Ronny seemed to. Pete put his arm round me then. "And I know you'd rather have him, sick though he is, than not have him at all. Am I right?" I nodded again. And I realised I didn't want this moment to end. I just wanted to stay here forever, with Pete and Ronny, in the comforting darkness of this little room.

***

The next day, Pete had to leave. The happiness of Christmas was over. I had that feeling again, that I'd had when the war first started. A sickness in my stomach. All we had to look forward to now was winter, and rationing, and fear of the Germans, and Pete wasn't even going to be there.

Chapter 6

Throughout the beginning of 1940, we kept hearing bad news on the wireless all the time. The Germans were getting closer. First they'd taken over Poland, then they'd started invading other countries. I kept hearing the word Blitzkrieg, but I didn't know what it meant, and Mum would just turn the wireless off. She didn't seem to hear some of my questions. She spent a lot of time looking out of the window. I was glad I lived in England, far away from the Germans, but I started to get very worried about Pete. And then we got a letter saying he was being moved to Norway.

Only Ronny could make me happy. He was growing up now. His legs looked too long for his body, but his feet were still big like a cub's. His growls sounded deeper, and sharp, like claws scratching stone. I loved him so much, and even though I still worried about him all the time until my stomach was sore and I couldn't sleep, I knew I would rather have him than not have him, just like Pete had said.

All the way through the winter there were no air-raids. And all the way through the spring, there were no air-raids. We thought the war would never come to us.

I was always reading any newspaper I could get my hands on, and Mr Florey usually had the Telegraph on his desk. When he'd finished with it, he tore it up and put it in the toilet to be used as toilet paper. So one way or another I got to read it. And I read one day that the Germans had invaded Norway.

I was nearly sick. All I could think of was Pete, fighting the Germans. Even Ronny couldn't stop me thinking of that. We had no idea if he was all right, until we got his letters. And even then, we knew his letters had been sent a week ago or more, so anything could have happened since he wrote them. Mum must have heard the news on the radio too, because when I got home, I could see she'd been crying. She was putting some wet washing through the ringer on the table. She smiled at me. "Hello, love," she said, as if nothing had happened. Then she sniffed.

"I read something in the paper, Mum," I said. "The Germans are in Norway, aren't they?"

Mum put the washing down. She took a big breath. Then she said to me, in a really strong voice, "Don't you go worrying about Pete. He can look after himself you know."

"I know," I said, and she put her arms around me.

"Now, you can give me a hand with this washing, love. And there's a pie in the oven. We'll have a lovely dinner. You're getting so thin."

I think I felt a bit better after that. But only for a while. I could tell Mum was only pretending to be happy. She kept singing whenever I was around. But sometimes, when she didn't know I was standing in the doorway, I saw her just staring out of the window, or at the picture of Pete on the sitting room mantelpiece, next to the picture of Dad. Sometimes I wished Dad could be with us, to hug Mum, and to put me on his shoulders, and make everything better.

***

One day, as Mr Florey and I stood in the public viewing hall, watching Ronny wandering around his enclosure, Mr Florey said to me, "He's getting to be a big lad, you know." I nodded. "They don't stay cubs forever do they?"

"No. I wish they did."

"You're going to have to be careful from now on."

I didn't say anything. "Do you know what I mean?"

"You mean, he could hurt me?"

"Yes. He wouldn't mean to of course. But... an adult tiger likes its privacy. They don't always want their friends so close, like cubs do."

"Don't they?"

"He's growing into a killer, Jill. He's not there yet. He's still a baby at heart. But you can't fight nature. You've been like his mother, but a mother lets her baby go when he's ready. That's the way they are made. It's how they think. When he's ready, he'll want to be on his own."

I watched him strolling about in the enclosure. He looked up at us, as if he knew we were talking about him. His eyes were dark, like Ronny the First's. Suddenly, I knew Mr Florey was right. Soon he wouldn't need me anymore.

I arrived home that night to find Mum sitting at the kitchen table. I knew something was wrong before I even saw her face. She was just sitting there, hardly moving. She hadn't lit the fire in the boiler, and the kitchen was freezing cold.

Then she looked up at me. When I saw her face, I realised she was crying. She was holding a piece of brown paper. It had to be a telegram. She didn't even try to hide it from me. I couldn't bring myself to walk towards her. I felt as if I was frozen in ice. Mum was gazing at me, her eyes filled with tears. She managed to speak. "He's not dead, just missing."

Chapter 7

Even now, after so many years have passed, I remember how dreadful I felt when I heard that news. I wanted to believe Pete was going to come home, that really he was all right. I tried to tell Mum he would walk in the door one day soon, but she shook her head and cried. It was as if suddenly the war had come right into our home. Until then, I had been scared of it, without really knowing what it could do. But at that moment, I saw that the war could take away the people I loved.

I slept in Mum's bed that night. I thought I would never be able to sleep, but I did, a bit. Every time I woke, Mum was awake too. Sometimes I'd find her crying quietly. I wanted to remind her that Pete was only missing, not gone forever, and that one day he'd be found and would come home. But I think I knew, deep down, that 'Missing in action' meant 'Probably dead.'

The next day, my two grans came to stay with us. They gave us great big hugs and cooked dinner for us. Granny Larch talked about what a wonderful boy Pete was, and how she was sure he'd be alright. She said he was probably hiding in a barn, being looked after by a pretty Norwegian lass. I liked that idea, and she said it with such conviction that I was sure she was probably right. It made me feel better for a while, but I knew it was just a story. Granny Crow said that we just had to be strong, pray for Pete and carry on as normal.

We got a lot of cards and letters from people who knew Pete. There was one from Mr Florey. It said he hoped I would come up to the zoo soon because he and Ronny were missing me. There was even a card from Doctor Barker. I didn't read that one.

When my grans had to go home, I went back to school. I didn't tell anyone about Pete. I just said I'd been ill. School helped me to forget about the war, except when we had air-raid practices. Ronny helped me forget too. But wherever I went, I wished Pete was with me. And every night, I prayed and wished that he would just come home. Mum said that not knowing made it worse. I even heard her saying to someone once, it would have been easier on us if they just told us he was dead. Mum was like a different person now. She shouldn't say things like that.

One Saturday, things got even worse.

When I got home, everything was normal for a

while. Mum had loads of washing strung up across the kitchen and she was on her hands and knees, scrubbing the floor.

"Hello, love," she said, sounding a bit surprised. "Is it that time already?"

"Yes," I said. There was a newspaper on the table. I saw photos of battle ships with huge clouds of smoke coming from them. I knew what had happened. Our headmaster had told us all about it in assembly. The British army had been brought back to England from Dunkirk Beach in France. They had nearly been beaten by the Germans, but hundreds of fishermen, and ordinary people with boats, had sailed across the sea to rescue them and bring them back. They'd brought lots of French soldiers too, because now the Germans had taken over France.

Some children said it was exciting, to think about such a daring rescue, but it wasn't exciting to me. My brother was missing. He might even be dead. Everything about the war was horrible. And now it was worse than ever because the Germans were winning. Would they come here next? They'd taken Pete away, and I was terrified they'd take my mum too, and maybe even Ronny.

Mum carried on scrubbing while I did some

homework at the cold table. When Mum saw me looking at the paper, she moved it away. When I finished my homework I helped Mum make dinner. We had to be careful not to use too many ingredients because everything was rationed now, but that was alright because I didn't really feel like eating much. When we'd washed the dishes, Mum lit the fire in the sitting room, and I played with my farm set on the floor. I really wanted to go and see Ronny, but I didn't want to leave Mum. Then, she said, "Come and sit with me, love. I want to talk to you." I did as she said. She put her arm round me and kissed me. Her eyes were red. "I've been thinking," she said. "I don't know about this war. I don't know if London's always going to be safe." I didn't know what to say. I felt scared. "I can't pretend to you, darling. I want to keep you safe, and happy. Children shouldn't have to worry about terrible things like war, but it's happening, love. We've lost Pete..." She put her hand over her mouth to stop herself crying. It didn't work. She pulled a handkerchief from her sleeve and dabbed her eyes. "Sorry love," she said. "But if the war does come to London, I don't want you here, in danger."

"What do you mean?" I asked.

"Well, you know how some of your friends at school have been evacuated?"

"Yes, Mum, but..."

"Well, I'm sure there are lots of very nice families in the countryside who would be lovely to live with."

"No, Mum," I said. "Please don't send me away!"

"The government are organising more evacuations. I want you to be safe, my darling. I've already lost one of my children to this war. I'm not going to let you be in any danger."

All I could think of was Ronny. Of course I didn't want to leave Mum either, but Ronny would be all alone. What if Doctor Barker decided to have him killed? What if bombs fell on him? I couldn't go away and leave him. He needed me. "I don't want to go," I said.

"I don't want to be away from you either, darling," she said. That made me feel bad. Mum thought I was sad about going away from her when really I was thinking about Ronny. "But you'll be very happy there. It'll be lovely in the countryside, I promise."

I begged my mum not to send me away, but she had made up her mind.

***

It was June when I went to the zoo to say goodbye to Ronny.

"Hello, Jill," Mr Florey said. I could tell by his voice something was wrong.

"Hello," I said, worried. "Is Ronny all right?"

"Yes, yes, he's fine." We were in the service corridor downstairs.

"Can I go in, then?"

Mr Florey looked over his spectacles at me.

"Jill, love," he said, and wiggled his nose a bit. "I..." Now I was really worried. Whatever he needed to tell me, he couldn't make himself say it. "I can't let you go in with him anymore."

"Wha...?" I shook my head.

"Doctor Barker says... He's right. You shouldn't go in with Ronny anymore."

"Why not?" I said. "I always go in with him. He wants me to."

"But... Remember what I said before, Jill. He's not a cub anymore. He's getting big now. He's growing up. Big tigers... Well, they're killers."

I couldn't believe it. I was so angry. I wouldn't let Doctor Barker stop me going to see my best friend. "I *hate* Doctor Barker. He doesn't understand," I said.

"But Jill," Mr Florey said. "He *does* understand. He's right, too. Ronny is your friend, but he's big enough to hurt you badly now."

"He wouldn't do that. He loves me."

"Yes, yes he does. But grown up tigers like to be left alone. They don't take kindly to having people following them round. I should have put a stop to it before. It's time to let go of him."

I put my hand over my mouth. Let go of him? He was my best friend, and I was his. We loved each other.

"I've come to say goodbye to him," I said, crying.

"I know that, love. I'm sorry. But Ronny'll understand, I'm sure."

But I knew Ronny wouldn't understand. He would wonder why I wasn't coming in to play with him. He would think I had stopped loving him. And when I went away, he would wonder why I had left him.

But I had no choice. I went round into the public viewing hall, and sat on one of the benches at the back, opposite the enclosures. There were quite a few people there, chattering and pointing and moving slowly along past the cheetah and the jaguar and the other big cats. Past Ronny. I had my chin on my hands, and I felt as if I couldn't move. I just stared through the crowd, at Ronny, who was gnawing on a huge bone. He looked up at me sometimes too. I wondered what he was thinking and I wished everyone would go away.

I stayed there for ages, ignoring the pins-and-needles in my hands, and the cold draft on my neck. Just before closing time, when the public area was empty, I got up and walked over to Ronny's enclosure. I leaned against the barrier. He was wandering about, all alone. Then he stopped and looked at me. I wondered if he was angry with me for not coming in. I wondered if he thought I didn't love him anymore. I smiled at him, and reached my hand forward. We stared at each other for what seemed like ages. Then, he walked off to the other end of his enclosure and lay down.

He had his back to me.

I waited, to see if he would look at me again, but he didn't. He licked his big paws. He was my best friend, but I was leaving him.

Chapter 8

There were hundreds of other children on the platform, saying goodbye to their mums. We all had big cardboard labels with our names on hanging on string round our necks, and our gas masks at our sides. We were being sent away to a little village a few miles outside London, called Belford. I was hot, because it was a warm day and I was wearing my thick, woollen coat and my woolly hat. They wouldn't fit in my case. I was holding my tiger teddy that Pete had given me for Christmas. I was standing with Mum and my grans. It reminded me of the day we had left Pete at the station, only this time I was the one leaving. The billeting officer, a tall woman I'd seen sometimes in school, announced something and waved her hands. All the children started to go towards her.

My mum hugged me and told me she loved me. But I was angry with her. She was making me hurt Ronny. I let her hug me but I didn't say anything and I didn't look at her. Granny Crow looked down at me and said, "Now, Jill. You know this is for your own good. Be nice to your mother."

"I don't want to go," I said.

"We wish you could stay too, my darling," said Granny Larch. "But it's not safe. Your mother is right. Please don't be angry."

But all I could think was, what if Ronny gets ill when I'm not there? What if Doctor Barker decides to have him killed? He would die without me and it would all be my mum's fault.

I hugged her because I didn't like my grans thinking I was rude. I thought, "I wish it was her who was going to die." But straight away I was furious with myself for thinking such a terrible thing. I knew I didn't wish that at all, and now I didn't want to let go of her, but I had to.

Soon, I was squashed into a carriage compartment with lots of other children. Some of them had been evacuated before, and some didn't want to go back. There was lots of talking. One girl was crying, but a bigger girl, older than me, was cuddling her. There were two little boys from my school. They were younger than me, and very scruffy. They didn't even have coats. They were on their own and they looked really scared. I tried to smile at them, but I couldn't make my face do that. I just hugged my teddy, and looked out of the window at my mum who was waving and smiling and crying. And the train slowly pulled away.

***

We had walked all round the village, from the tiny station, down all the stony streets of little cottages, and back onto the main road. It was so quiet. There were very few cars, and they didn't have trolley buses or taxis here. Just a few people walking, or on bikes or horses. The whole place seemed to smell of horse droppings, which reminded me of the zoo.

There were only a few houses left now. Lots of children had already been chosen, but there were still a few of us waiting to be given somewhere to stay. The two younger boys from my school were still there, and they had never seen cows and sheep before. When a flock of sheep came past us, the boys leapt up onto a garden wall. Myself and a girl about my age, called Ruby, giggled about it. But we were just as confused as the boys when we saw the stripy cows.

"Never knew cows could have stripes," Ruby said.

I thought I knew all about weird animals, but I'd never seen that before. A herd of brown cows, each with three white stripes down their sides!

"Everything has stripes these days," said the billeting officer, a tall, dark haired lady with big round spectacles and a quiet voice. "Even the cows. To make them show up better in the blackout. Can't have people crashing their cars into errant cows now can we?" We shook our heads.

A few minutes later, we were at the gate of a small brick cottage.

The billeting officer went to the door and knocked. The door opened, and I saw a thin lady, with straggly hair that was going a bit grey.

"Hello, Glyn," she said.

"Hello June, how are you?"

"Tired," she said. "Bloomin' baby won't stop crying. You look busy."

"Oh yes. Walked the length and breadth of the town. Got a few left. Will you take one?"

She didn't look friendly and I hoped she'd say no. Mum had said she would make sure I was put with someone nice, but that wasn't how it worked.

"Well I'll have to," she replied. "It's the law, ent it?" The billeting officer nodded. The lady stepped out of her house. She was wearing a skirt and an apron, and a thin set of pearls round her neck. She studied us all. I looked at the ground, hoping she wouldn't notice me.

"I'll take her," she said.

Please let her be pointing at someone else.

I looked up. No. Her bony finger was waving right at me. She smiled at me, but it didn't last long.

I didn't want to move. Some of the other billeters had seemed really nice. Why did I have to have this one?

The billeting officer told her my name, even though it was written on the label I was wearing. "And this is Mrs Hill," she said to me. "I'm sure you'll be very happy here. She's a good friend of mine." Trying to look cheerful, I said goodbye and good luck to the others, and followed the lady up the path. I smiled at her. But really I was missing my mum already. And Ronny too, and Pete of course. There was a huge lump in my throat now and I hoped I wouldn't have to speak yet, because I didn't think I could.

I could hear a baby crying inside the house. Mrs Hill and the billeting officer spoke for a little while. Then she led me inside. There was a strong smell that I didn't like, or recognise. It made me want to screw up my nose, but that would be rude so I tried not to. She took me into the kitchen at the back of the house. There was a big table, and on it there was a baby in a basket. It was crying loudly, but Mrs Hill ignored it. Looking round, I saw there was a long cooking range instead of an electric cooker. There was a big brass bucket of coal next to it. An old, tall mangle, like a big version of our wringer, stood in the corner.

The back door was open, and I could see a long garden, enclosed by an ivy-covered brick wall. In places, forests of high stinging nettles grew against the wall, and at the end of the garden was a large, grassy mound, with a metal front and a low door. It was an Anderson shelter. Next to it was the outhouse, and a coal bunker and a small stack of wood.

I was still holding my case, and it was really heavy but I didn't want to put it down without being told to. Mrs Hill opened the range door and gave the fire a poke. There were some vegetables on the side which she had started to cut up. She laid a towel over them to stop flies landing on them, then turned to me.

"Right, I'll show you where to put your things," she said. She still sounded cross, and I wondered if I had done something wrong. She led me back into the small, narrow hallway. On one side, there was a door to a front room but we didn't go in. Instead, she went up the steep, dark stairs, and I followed her. Upstairs, there were two more doors leading off the landing, and the wooden floor was all wonky and creaky.

"Right," she said, "that door there, you don't go in." It must have been her bedroom. "This door here is the boys' bedroom. You can't sleep in there, there ent room. But you'll have to keep your clothes in there." She led me inside. It was so messy I couldn't believe my eyes. There were three beds, all unmade. One was a proper bed. The other two were just mattresses and sheets on the floor. There were piles of rocks and old bits of wood all over the place. There were some school books scattered around the floor, an open box of matches, a rusty kitchen knife, some nails and a hammer, and a brick, all lying on the floorboards or mixed up in the bed sheets. The room smelt musty, even though the little back window was open wide. At least the baby's crying was quieter here.

"You'll put your things in this drawer," Mrs Hill said. She pulled open the bottom drawer in the old chest under the window. "I'll be in the kitchen when you're done." She left the room, and I stood there, not wanting to touch anything. The whole house seemed to creak as she went down the stairs. The roof was high in the middle, but where it sloped downwards, it was too low even for me to stand up straight. There were models of planes hanging on string from the beams, and more models on the little desk in the corner. There were large black patches on the walls where mould had started to make the paint peel. I didn't want to be there. I wondered how many boys there were who lived in this room. I wished I was at home with Mum and I kept thinking about how unkind I'd been to her at the station.

Eventually, I unpacked my case and put my clothes in the drawer. It was only big enough for some of my clothes, so I left the rest in the case, and stood it against the wall. I hoped that would be alright with Mrs Hill. I tucked my teddy in there too. Hoping the boys would not touch my things, I took my coat off, and put it on top of my case, folded. I put the big label on top of it too. I put my gas mask box back on though.

I went back down the stairs. Mrs Hill was stirring something in a pan, and rocking the baby's basket. She was doing it too fast. Even I knew you couldn't stop a baby crying by rocking it like that. I wanted to ask where I was going to sleep. I was so grateful I wasn't going to be sleeping in the boys' room. But I still couldn't speak. If I had tried, I knew I would have just cried.

Mrs Hill ignored me for ages. I didn't even know if she knew I was there, so I made a little coughing noise. She said, "Can't you see I'm doing two things at once? You can rock a baby, can't you?" I nodded and hurried to where she was standing. I rocked the baby for her, slowly. It didn't make any difference, it still cried so loud it made my ears hurt. Mrs Hill was smoking a cigarette. She tapped it so the burnt bit fell off onto the stone floor. The food she was cooking did smell nice, but the cigarette smoke made my throat sting. I peered at the baby. It's face was all screwed up. I didn't know if it was a boy or a girl. I could tell it was probably hungry though, or needed its nappy changed.

Just then, I saw two boys run into the back garden through the gate at the far end. They looked younger than me. They were both filthy, with long hair sticking up in every direction, and old shirts all torn. They were waving big sticks and shouting something about the Germans. They had a quick fight in the garden, and one of them pretended to die. Then they both got up and ran into the kitchen. They ran right through, pushing past me, shouting again, and I heard them going upstairs. I could still hear them shouting and fighting even when they got into their room. Mrs Hill didn't even seem to notice them. But she did tut when she saw the muddy footprints on the kitchen floor.

"I'm glad I got a girl," she said after a while. She didn't look at me though. I carried on rocking the baby. "Boy are so messy," she said. "Can't get 'em to tidy up for love nor money. But you'll help me, won't you love." She turned to look at me now. I nodded, and tried to smile. I wanted to say, "Of course I will," but as soon as I opened my mouth I felt my chin start to shake and the lump in my throat got bigger. I closed my mouth, and carried on nodding. "Good. There's a broom in the closet over there. Be a good girl and sweep up the mess. No, tell you what. Baby needs changing first. God, he'll be the death of me with that scream of his. You changed a nappy before?" I shook my head. "Well, it's not difficult. Just make sure you don't stick the pin into him. You'll find everything in the front room. Don't go touching anything else, mind. Can you carry him yourself? You look good 'n' strong."

I lifted the basket down. It was heavy, and I had

to use both hands, but I managed. "You can do the floor when you've finished him," Mrs Hill said, and turned back to her cooking. I took the baby into the front room. This was where the horrible smell was coming from. It was so bad in here I nearly choked. I quickly climbed onto the messy bed which was against the wall under the open window. I breathed the air from outside. The smell in this room was dirty nappies. I realised there were lots of them in a metal bucket in the corner. The rest of the room was as messy as the boys' room upstairs. There were piles of clothes, adult's and baby's. A pair of blue dungarees was lying screwed up on the floor, all covered in dirt and straw. There were towels and socks on a drying-rack in front of the fire place, even though the fire hadn't been lit. There was a pair of muddy Wellington boots, and footprints on the floorboards and the rug. There was an empty jug on the floor, and, I realised with disgust, there was an old fashioned chamber pot, which had been used and hadn't been emptied. Not a child's potty, but a proper adult's chamber pot! I wanted to run away.

The baby was still screaming.

I took him out of the basket and laid him down on a grubby towel. I undid the pin and opened the nappy. The smell nearly made me sick, and then I realised I didn't have anything to clean him with. I didn't know how to change a nappy. I'd never even seen anyone else do it. But I could see I would have to wipe him. There wasn't any water here, so I went back into the kitchen.

"I don't know what to wipe him with," I said. It was the first time I had actually spoken to Mrs Hill, and my voice came out all quiet.

"Just use the nappy," Mrs Hill said. "Fold his doings up inside it, and wipe him with the outside. There's a jar of Vaseline in there. Put some of that on before you put his clean nappy on. Do you know how to put a nappy on him?"

I shook my head. She tutted, and put out her cigarette. "I suppose I'll have to come and show you then. I hope you're a quick learner 'cause I ent got time to show you every time." She came into the front room. "Bloody 'ell," she said when she smelt the stink. "You'll have to take that bucket out an' all when you're done." But she didn't notice the chamber pot.

She showed me how to clean the baby up, and how to put Vaseline all over the red, sore patches where his nappy went. Then she showed me how to put the new nappy on him. The difficult bit was the pin. I was so scared I would stick it into him. The baby screamed the whole time, and didn't even stop when she put him back in his basket.

After that, I took the bucket of nappies outside and stood it by the back door. I wondered what she was going to do with them, if she was going to expect me to scrub them clean. She didn't say anything though, so I quickly made a start on sweeping the kitchen floor. I was relieved Mrs Hill hadn't noticed the chamber pot in the other room. I was sure she'd have made me empty it if she had. All afternoon she had jobs for me. I had to scrub the hall floor, beat the rugs and hang the washing on the line and fetch some coal and wood in. I began to wonder if I would ever be allowed to sit down and play, or read, or write letters. Then I realised Mrs Hill hadn't showed me where I was going to sleep. I'd seen the whole house, and there weren't any spare beds. I was too scared to ask though.

The baby was asleep in the smelly front room now. I helped Mrs Hill lay the table. There were four big chairs, two smaller chairs with torn cushions on them, and a high, wobbly stool at the far end. Mrs Hill called the two boys over and over again before they came. I could tell they were twins, even though they weren't identical. They both had chubby, freckly faces, and their messy blonde hair was full of dirt and leaves. It looked as if they were wearing their school clothes, even though it was a Saturday, and their knees were all bruised and cut. They were fighting as they came into the kitchen and Mrs Hill gave them both a hard smack round the head. They didn't seem to care though. She sent them out into the garden to wash their hands in the bucket by the door. Then they came back in, leaving footprints on my clean floor, and sat at the table. I noticed their wet hands were still covered in dirt. Mrs Hill had made me sit on the stool. I felt ridiculous; it was so high my knees wouldn't go under the table. The boys looked up at me curiously.

"Who's she?" one of them said, as if he'd only just noticed me.

"She's the girl from the city," Mrs Hill said. "Go on, introduce yourselves."

I smiled at them. One of them said, "What's yer name then?"

"Why'd we have to have a girl?" the other one said.

"Now now, don't be so rude to guests," Mrs Hill said. "Her name's..." She looked at me. "What did you say your name is?"

"Jill."

"I hate girls," one of the boys said.

"Tell her your names, and stop being rude," Mrs Hill said.

"I'm Joe."

"I'm George."

They both looked at each other and laughed.

"That's enough, the both of you. Where the hell have the others got to?" She put a big pie in the middle of the table, and looked at the clock on the wall. "Said they'd be home by now. I did tell 'em I was cooking pie." I hadn't realised I was starving until then, and the smell of the pie made my tummy growl like Ronny.

"Mmm, pie!" said Joe. Or George. I had already forgotten which was which. "Girls can't have pie!"

Mrs Hill hit him round the head and some of the grass from his hair fell onto his plate. I winced, but the boy didn't seem to mind getting hit. Then the front door opened. In came a tall, thin boy, older than me, but not as old as Pete. He was wearing a shirt and trousers held up with braces. "Smells good, Ma," he called. "Thought I might have missed it."

"Just in time, love," Mrs Hill replied. "I thought

you'd be here by now."

"Well I am," he said, coming into the kitchen.

"Hold your nose, Tim," one of the twins said, "there's a girl here!" They laughed until Tim grabbed each of them by an ear. He twisted them so hard that both boys stood up, squealing, and going red in the face. I was about to beg him to stop. "Don't be so 'orrible, you pair of little rats," Tim said. Then he let them go. They sat down rubbing their ears and looking really angry. One of them looked as if he was about to cry. Mrs Hill didn't seem to mind that Tim had hurt them like that.

Tim looked at me as he sat down. He had a big nose and lots of red spots all over his narrow face. "Hello," he said. "I'm Tim. What's your name?"

"Jill," I said.

"Don't take no notice of my brothers. They don't know how to behave." I smiled.

"Now you're here, Tim," Mrs Hill said, "you can say grace."

"Alright, now that I'm the man of the house." He cleared his throat and everyone put their hands together. I did the same. "Lord, thanks for all this lovely food you've put upon our table. I'll eat it all and then I'll fart as loud as I am able." The twins were roaring with laughter before he'd even finished. I smiled too. It *was* funny. Mrs Hill looked cross.

"Tim," she said. "A proper one."

"Alright, alright." We all put our hands together again. "Soggy cabbage, stringy meat on every bloomin' plateful—" The boys were screaming with laughter again, "—For what we all must now endure, Lord make us truly grateful."

I giggled.

Mrs Hill sighed, and said quickly, "For what we are about to receive, may the lord make us truly thankful. Amen. Right. Pie everyone?"

Chapter 9

Tim did remind me of Pete sometimes. But thinking about Pete made me feel lonely and frightened. What had happened to him? Mum was right, not knowing did make it hard to bear, but it was better than hearing he was dead. Mrs Hill made me do all the dishes while she sat at the kitchen table, smoking and talking to Tim about what was happening in the war. Tim's father had gone off to join the fighting, and was somewhere in Africa. Tim and Mrs Hill were really worried about him, but, I thought, at least they knew he was still alive. Tim said he thought the Germans might be going to win the war. If they were, I wished they'd just get on with it so it could all be over.

It was Saturday night, and we'd be going to church tomorrow, so when I'd dried all the dishes and put them away in the cupboard, and changed the baby's nappy again, and swept the kitchen floor, Mrs Hill said it was bath time.

Tim put the tub on the floor and helped Mrs Hill fill it with kettlefuls of hot water from the range. Then we took it in turns to have our baths. We all had to go out of the kitchen while Mrs Hill had hers. The boys went to their room. They were supposed to be doing their homework, but they weren't. I could hear them playing and fighting, even Tim. I was worried they'd wake the baby, who was now fast asleep in the front room. I didn't have a room to go to, so I sat on the stairs. Granny Larch had bought me some comics, but they were in my case upstairs, and I didn't want to go into the boys' room while they were all there.

We all used the same bath water. I had to go last, and it was cold and dirty by then. Mrs Hill scrubbed everyone's backs with a big wooden brush. She even did mine. It hurt.

When everyone was bathed, and the tub emptied and hung up on the wall outside, Mrs Hill went upstairs, and came back down with some blankets and a small cushion. I was really tired, but I still didn't know where I was going to sleep.

"We ent got any spare beds," she said to me. "You'll have to sleep under the table. You'll be comfy enough, I'm sure." The kitchen floor was covered in red flagstones. It would be cold and hard. I didn't know why she thought it would be comfy.

I put the blankets on the floor under the table and lay down there. I'd used all the blankets to make a mattress, so I didn't have anything to put over the top of me. I used my dressing gown as a blanket, and put a jumper on over my nightdress.

The blackout curtains made it really dark. The fire in the range was glowing a little bit, but that was all I could see. I wished I was with Mum or Pete. I missed them both worse than ever now. The darkness was full of noises I didn't recognise, and my mind kept playing tricks on me. Every creak and thump was something horrible, watching me, coming closer... I'd never been scared of the dark before, but I'd always had Mum and Pete close to me. Now they were far away.

Trying not to think about that, I wondered who slept in the front room bed. Even though that room stank, I wished I could have had the bed. My tiger-teddy that Pete had given me for Christmas was in my case upstairs, but I didn't want to go up and get it, even though I really wanted to hold it and pretend it was the real Ronny. There was a cold draft from under the door and I didn't think I'd be able to sleep, but I did.

Angry voices woke me up suddenly in the night though. I lay there terrified for a while, hardly daring to open my eyes, before I realised what it was. There was an argument going on in the hall way. The kitchen door was partly open and, in the glow from a candle or an oil lamp, I could just see the dark shape of someone I hadn't met.

"You can't tell me what to do, you bossy cow!" the young woman was shouting. "I ent done nothing wrong!"

"Ent done nothing wrong?" Mrs Hill shouted back. "Ent done nothing wrong? You got a baby in there, spent the whole day crying for you!"

"You said *you'd* look after 'im!"

"Didn't know you were going to be out all night, did I! You need to learn some responsibility, girl."

"What, ent I entitled to a day off every once in a while? I work my fingers to the bone on that farm. It ent easy work. It's men's work."

"You spend the whole day flirting with the fellers up there, more like."

"Fellers? What fellers? They're all off fighting, Mum."

"Not all of them."

"Well I ent gonna be interested in the ones that's left, am I. One's got a gammy leg and the other one's half blind!"

"Don't exaggerate, girl. If your Patrick knew the way you carried on with those boys..."

"Oh leave it, Mum. He probably found himself a

nice French girl or two anyway."

"He's not even *in* France anymore! He's back in England now."

"Yes, but God knows where."

I turned onto my back. My hip was hurting where it had been pressing into the ground. I wished I had a pillow. The row carried on for a while. But then the front room door slammed, and I heard Mrs Hill going back upstairs.

***

The next morning, it was already light when I woke up. My body hurt all over from my uncomfortable bed. There was someone in the kitchen. It was a woman with long, blonde hair. She was wearing a red dressing gown and slippers. I could smell cigarette smoke. She was just standing there, looking out of the window. Then the kettle started to whistle. I wondered if she knew I was there. I wondered if I should introduce myself. She sighed, and took the kettle off the stove.

I leaned out from under the table. "Hello," I said.

"Ruddy 'ell! What the blazes?" She turned and looked down at me. Her face was pale, and she had thick, dark make up on her eyes, though a lot of it had run down her cheeks. "Who on Earth are you?" she said, sucking her cigarette. "Nearly made me drop the kettle! What are you doing there?" I could tell from her voice she was the one who had been arguing with Mrs Hill last night.

"I'm Jill. I'm from London. I've been sent here while the war is on, in case the Germans drop bombs on London."

"Oh, an evacuee. Mum said we'd probably be getting one. Well, come on out then, I won't bite you." I came out and stood in front of her. She looked at me for ages. "Just what we need, another kid," she said. "Well, I suppose you'll have your uses. Do you drink tea?" I nodded, and wondered if that meant she was going to make me one. "Sit down," she said. She sounded a bit cross, like Mrs Hill did. I was cold, but she'd got the range fire going so I sat on a chair beside it and warmed my hands. She put the tea pot on the table and let it stew for a while.

"I'm Mary," she said.

"Pleased to meet you," I said, and she laughed.

"You always so polite?"

I said, "Mum tells me it's important to be polite."

"Ooh, does she now?" Mary said in a pretend

posh voice. "Well you ent gonna like it here then." I felt the lump coming back into my throat when I remembered my mum, and how I'd been horrid to her at the station. Mary making fun of her made me feel worse. I waited until she turned away to get the cups before I wiped the tears from my eyes.

She made me tea and I sipped it. It didn't have any milk in it but the hot cup felt nice in my hands.

I could hear the baby starting to cry in the front room. Mary tutted. "Ruddy 'ell. I never get any peace. Can you cook?"

"Er... yes," I said. "I help my mum a lot."

"Good, 'cause they'll all be down soon wanting their breakfast. Mum won't get up if she knows us two are down here, and I've got to go and feed '*im*, so you'll have to do it. Know what to do with powdered egg?" I nodded. "There's milk outside in a bucket of water. Should be alright still. Make a big pot of tea, and toast some bread over the fire. There's a toasting fork on the wall there. There's jam and butter in the larder. Not too much mind, it's rationed. And it's Sunday, so use the china." She pointed to the shelf where all the china cups and plates were stacked. "Alright?"

"I nodded."

"I'll have to help you if you get stuck." The baby

was crying loudly now. "You know where I'll be." And she went out of the kitchen. I heard the front room door close. Soon the baby's crying stopped. I wished Mum would just come and take me away. I wished I could be holding Ronny, rubbing his fur, and letting him curl up on my lap like he used to. He was much too big for that now though.

I made breakfast like Mary said. Mrs Hill kept on complaining I hadn't put things in the right place, or I hadn't made the tea hot enough, or done the egg right. The boys didn't seem to mind though. Tim said grace, but he didn't do a funny one. He did wink at me though when Mrs Hill said the toast was too black on one side. I think he thought she was too strict.

She made me wash all the dishes, but she did dry them up herself and put them away. Then we had to go to church. Mrs Hill washed the boys' hands and faces with cold water. Then she did the same to mine. She was rough, and the flannel smelt of mould and dirt. Even when she'd finished, and dried us, I could still smell it on my skin. She told me to put my best dress on, and made the boys stay out of their room for a few minutes so I could change in there. Wearing that dress reminded me of the day Mum had come to the zoo to meet

Ronny, and we'd met Mr Kendal, the wolf-man. I wished it could be that day again.

Chapter 10

It was drizzling. The church was small and dark, and cold. Just like everywhere else, it had thick blackout curtains. Inside, on the walls, there were some posters which looked as if they didn't belong in a church. They were about the war. One had the words 'Make do and mend', and another said 'Mum's the word'. I didn't understand that one, but just seeing it suddenly made me miss my mum more than ever. I could see some of the children who had been on the same train as me. The two little boys were there, and the girl who had been crying. I don't think they saw me though. The vicar was a young man, and he made us pray for all the soldiers. He also said that everyone in the village was honoured to be looking after children from the city, and that in this time of war, everyone must help everyone else. I wondered if he meant that we evacuees must help our families with all the housework.

That afternoon, Mrs Hill told me about my new school. She said I would go with the boys. They would show me where I had to go. I didn't want to go to school, but at least I might be able to relax a bit there. I would have play time and dinner time all to myself. I wanted to write a letter to Mum. I didn't feel cross with her anymore. I wanted to tell her I loved her. And I would ask her to go and see Ronny for me, and tell him I loved him too.

***

Mrs Hill always made me do housework. None of the other children had to do it. I felt angry sometimes, but I knew I mustn't show it because I had seen how furious she had been with Mary that night and I didn't want her to be like that with me. Besides, even though she never smiled and was always a bit cross, I did almost feel sorry for her.

But I used my dinner times and play times in school to write my letters. I wrote to my mum twice a week. At first, I tried to tell her how awful it was here, and she said she was so sorry for sending me. She said I had to be strong, and to understand that she loved me and that London was not a safe place for me to be. But she wouldn't let me come home, not now that the Germans were so close. Besides, I think she just thought I was exaggerating because I was homesick. So, I decided not to write much about life with the Hills, and to concentrate more on what was happening at school instead. When she wrote to me, which she did twice a week too, she always sent me a new envelope with a stamp on it for my letter back to her. Sometimes she sent me a spare stamp, in case I wanted to write to anyone else. Sometimes she sent me a bit of money, for a treat, and even a little present. Once she sent me a small wooden tiger, just like the one I had sent to Pete for Christmas. I loved it, and I decided to hide it away in my case upstairs. I didn't want to lose it while I was running errands, and I thought that if it was safe, somehow that might mean Pete was too.

I also wrote to Mr Florey, to find out how Ronny was. But I wrote him two or three letters before I got a reply. I remember how excited I was when I got it. Tim gave it to me at breakfast, but I had to wait until dinner time in school before I had the chance to read it.

I sat in a corner of the long, brick air-raid shelter at the end of the playing field. It always smelt of wee in there, but I didn't care. It was the one place I could be alone. It was quite dark, but I could still read his curly handwriting. It said, "Dear Jill, I'm so sorry I haven't replied to your lovely letters until now. These cats don't half know how to keep me busy, I can tell you!" He told me all about what had been going on in the zoo, all the new animals that had been bought by the different houses, and all the animals that had been moved to Whipsnade, or other zoos, to keep them safe. They were evacuees, just like me! I liked hearing about all that, but it wasn't what I really wanted to know. In my letters to him, I had begged him to tell me how Ronny was, but in his he hardly mentioned him. Just before the end of his letter, he had written, "You won't believe how big Ronny is now. He's a real beauty. I told him you had sent your love, and I could tell that made him happy." Then the letter finished with, "Please write again. Your friend, Mr Florey."

Why hadn't he told me that Ronny was healthy and strong now, and that he wouldn't need his medicine for much longer? Why hadn't he told me Ronny was safe now, that Doctor Barker would never have to have him shot? Doctor Barker's words rang inside my head as clearly as if I had just heard them: "I'm afraid if he doesn't start showing an improvement soon, he will be K.B.O. That means killed by order. My order."

I decided to write another letter to Mr Florey. I would tell him I wanted to know the truth, no matter how terrible it was. At least if I knew about it, I could try and help.

It was another few days before I got my letter finished and sent. But it was much longer than that before I got a reply. Every morning I would listen for the post man. My heart would speed up and my throat would feel tight when he dropped letters through the door. Sometimes he never came, sometimes he would come during the day when I was at school. I was always excited to get my mum's letters of course, but why didn't Mr Florey write to me? Every day, I felt first excited and scared, then disappointed when there was nothing from him. Sometimes I wanted to cry, and sometimes I felt so furious with him I wanted to scream. What was happening to Ronny? Why wouldn't he tell me?

Chapter 11

It was the summer holidays before I saw my mum. She came to visit, but she couldn't stay the night because there wasn't enough space. I was hoping she would see how many jobs Mrs Hill made me do, and take me home with her. Mrs Hill came with me to meet her at the station. It was a little station with just one platform and a waiting room. We were the only people there when the train arrived. Soon, Mum was stepping down from the carriage, into the cloud of smoke and steam.

"Mum," I cried.

"Oh, Jill!" She ran and hugged me. I could smell her lovely perfume and her clean hair. I wondered what I smelt like. I knew my hair badly needed washing and combing.

"Hello, Mrs Larch," said Mrs Hill.

"Call me Joanna," Mum said.

"I'm June," Mrs Hill told her.

They shook hands and smiled at each other. I had hardly ever seen Mrs Hill smile before. Never, in fact. Mum looked at me again. She stroked my hair. "You've really grown, love," she said. "They must be feeding you well."

We went for a walk around the village. I knew it well by now, but Mrs Hill came with us anyway. She kept talking and was being really friendly. She was like a different person, but I wanted to be on my own with my mum.

"If you have things to do, June," Mum said, "I think Jill and I will be fine, won't we Jill?" But Mrs Hill smiled and said she had nothing to get back for, so we all walked down through the meadows and along the river. The blue sky was cluttered with bright white clouds, but it was still sunny and warm. I held Mum's hand all the time. Sometimes, when the overgrown path was narrow, Mrs Hill had to walk behind us.

"I've just realised," Mum said, as we stood on an old wooden bridge over the river. "No barrage balloons!"

"People don't really bother with gas masks here, either," I said, looking at mum's that was hanging at her side.

"Some days," Mrs Hill said, "you'd hardly know there was a war on." But I knew that until Pete came back, Mum and I would never forget about the war. Mum hugged me, as if she knew what I was thinking.

We went back to the house at lunch time. It was

really tidy in the hallway and kitchen, because Mrs Hill and I had spent Friday evening tidying up. There were no horrid smells today. I could hear Joe and George playing upstairs.

"You two sit down while I get lunch on the table," Mrs Hill said. But, out of habit, I started getting plates down. I was scared she would be cross with me later if I didn't. Mum said, "Would you like some help, June?"

"No, no, you sit down. Both of you." She nodded to me, so I did. "She's so helpful, this young lady," she said, smiling at my mum and patting my head.

We had bread and cheese and cold meat.

"Are the boys coming to join us?" Mum asked.

"Oh, no," said Mrs Hill. "Let's have some peace and quiet!" She laughed at herself, and Mum smiled.

Later, we decided to go for another walk. Mrs Hill said she'd come and show us the old mill, but Mum said, "Actually, June, if you don't mind I'd like to spend a bit of time on my own with Jill."

"Oh," Mrs Hill said. She seemed a bit hurt. "Of course. Have a lovely time."

We went to the Post Office where Tim worked. Mum wanted to meet him. Tim went a bit red when we walked in. "Hello, Mrs Larch," he said.

We chatted with him for a little while, and then we went to look at the church. There was a bench in the church yard and we sat down. I leant against her, and she put her arm round me.

"Tell me, darling," she said. "Are you... alright here?"

"Yes," I said, but I didn't look at her.

"Really?" She sounded like she didn't believe me.

"Well, I wish I could come home with you." I could feel my chin starting to crumple.

She kissed my head. "Mrs Hill seems nice. I know it was difficult at first, but... Does she look after you well?"

"Yes... I still have to do lots of jobs though."

"What sort of jobs, darling?"

"Just... making breakfast. And washing up and putting the things away."

"Well, you've had plenty of practice at that!"

"Yes. I have to clean the floor too. And beat the rugs, and change the baby's nappy, and feed the baby sometimes, and..." I couldn't keep speaking in case I cried. Mum hugged me. She took hold of my hand and looked at the sores on my fingers.

"I'd take you back with me if I could. I hate you not being with me. But the war is coming this way. Even if you have to do lots of chores, you are much safer here, my love. We don't know what's going to happen but... These are awful times. But you're my only child now, darling. I have to keep you safe."

I nodded. There was no way Mum would let me come home. I looked up and saw tears in her eyes. I knew she was remembering Pete.

"I miss him so much too, Mum," I said. She got a handkerchief out of her sleeve and dabbed her eyes, and then mine.

"This war's already taken half of everything I love in this world," she said. "I have to protect the other half no matter what." She stroked my hair, and we sat together for ages, not saying anything. We were both thinking about Pete, and I could tell Mum was feeling worse than she tried to let on. She had been really happy and cheerful all day, but now she was quiet. It reminded me of times at home when she was thinking of Dad. She'd be singing and smiling more than ever, but then we'd find her sitting in her chair by the fire, holding a photo of him, dabbing her eyes with a hanky.

Later, she plaited my hair for me. I hadn't had time to do it for ages. It had become a terrible mess. I loved sitting there in the church yard, smelling the warm, wet grass, and feeling my mum's gentle hands plaiting my hair. I wanted to say sorry that I hadn't washed it, but it didn't seem to matter.

In my stomach there was always a sick feeling, an ache. Some of it was for Pete, and some was for Ronny. I wished Mr Florey would reply to my letter.

"Mum," I said.

"Yes, honey."

"Could you do something for me when you get back to London?"

"Of course."

"Could you go to the zoo, and see Mr Florey for me? I want you to ask him to write to me." I told her about my letter.

"Of course I will," Mum said. "But don't worry too much. Maybe his letter has got lost in the post. It happens you know. A lot more now, too, since so many of the workers have gone to join the fighting."

I nodded, but I wondered if Mum was just trying to cheer me up. After all, *her* letters always got here.

***

When we got back to the house there was a lovely

smell of roasting chicken. "I hope you've worked up an appetite," Mrs Hill said.

The whole family came in for dinner. The boys didn't mess around at all, and Mary didn't swear. She even talked, quite politely, to my mum, telling her all about her farm duties as a Land Girl. She had to work hard, getting up early in the morning and finishing late. Mum seemed to like Mary, and I wondered if maybe she wasn't so bad after all. Mrs Hill told Mum that all the vegetables on the table were home grown, in the garden. They had a good crop of marrows and cabbages on top of the Anderson shelter, and potatoes, beans and all kinds of other vegetables on the patches either side of the path. Tim usually took care of them. Mrs Hill said he had green fingers, and Tim looked at his hands with a pretend worried frown. "I ent," he said, and everyone laughed.

I didn't have to help, even with the clearing up afterwards. When everyone had gone again, except us and Mrs Hill, Mum said to me, "Jill, darling, why don't you just pop along and play for a minute."

"But I..."

"June and I are going to have a chat." Mrs Hill was just pouring out another cup of tea. She stopped and looked at my mum.

I nodded, and got down from my chair. I pulled the kitchen door closed behind me. The baby was crying in the front room, and the boys were making a lot of noise upstairs. I sat on the bottom step. I could hear Mum's voice but I couldn't tell what she was saying. I couldn't hear Mrs Hill's voice at all. After a while, the door opened and Mum called me back in. Mrs Hill looked a bit red now. She smiled at me though and we had another cup of tea. Actually, it was only hot water and a sprinkle of powdered milk, as tea was rationed, but we still called it tea. When it was time for Mum to go, I said I'd walk her to the station. It was getting dark but Mum said it would be alright. Mum gave Mrs Hill a hug, and said, "Thanks for everything."

We walked really slowly through the village, and Mum held my hand all the way. I didn't ask what she and Mrs Hill had talked about, because I thought I already knew.

It was getting dark, but the sky was still bright orange behind the church. "You know," Mum said, "you can tell me anything. Anything at all. I will write to you every week. I'll send you money when I can so you can buy sweets and things. Clothes, too, or anything you need."

"Thanks," I said. Then we heard a strange noise, like a moaning sound. It was quiet at first. We stood still and listened. It got louder. It sounded more like a buzz now, coming from the sky. Aeroplanes. We couldn't see them because the sky was mostly dark. There were no air-raid sirens though. "Must be ours," Mum said. She hugged me. "It'll be alright. You'll be safe out here, you know. Why would the Germans want to drop bombs on this little place?" We carried on walking. Mum said that if the Germans didn't come maybe I'd be able to come back to London for a visit. Maybe I'd be able to see Ronny too.

When we got to the station we sat and waited for the train. "Promise me you'll run all the way back," Mum said.

I promised.

The noisy train came hissing and steaming into the station. The light on the front dazzled me as it went by. Mum stood, hugged me and kissed me.

"Remember to go and see Mr Florey," I said.

"Of course, my love."

And then she had to go.

***

As soon as I got in, I could tell Mrs Hill was cross with me. I didn't know what I had done to upset her. She was cleaning the table really hard, and her face was red.

"Oh yer back are yer?" She didn't look at me.

I stood in the kitchen doorway.

"Well are you going to help me then, or are you too good for a bit of housework?" She spat a bit as she said it.

"What would you like me to do?" I said quietly.

She had lots of things for me to do. I wanted to say no, and tell her to stop being so horrid, but that would just make things worse. And besides, Mum always taught me to respect my elders.

When I got to bed I was more tired and sore than ever.

Chapter 12

That night, I lay under the table trying to sleep. Even though it was still not properly dark outside, with the blackout curtains drawn it was totally dark inside. I was too hot, but at least I could use all my blankets to lie on, and my dressing gown as a pillow. I felt weak inside. And I felt silly for being scared of the dark, but it had never been this dark at night before. I was holding my tiger-teddy tonight. I never wanted to let go of it.

I cried for Pete. I couldn't believe he was dead, but I knew that's what Mum believed, so maybe he was. Sometimes, I even wished I was dead, so I could be with him. But then I wouldn't have Ronny or Mum. There was no way to make things right again. Even in my imagination.

The kitchen door opened. It was Mary, carrying a candle stick. She was wearing one of her pretty skirts, but she didn't have her high heeled shoes on yet. She must have thought I was asleep. She walked quietly and softly. She bent down and peered at me, and I quickly closed my eyes. When I looked again, she was getting something down from a shelf. It was a small tin. She put it on the side, and took the lid off. She took something out. I could hear the noise it made, like paper. There was the jangle of metal too. She looked around, and then crouched down to peer at me again. I closed my eyes, but I wasn't sure I'd done it quick enough this time. I kept them closed for ages. I felt the warmth of the candle on my face and I could see its light through my eyelids. She must have held it close to me, checking I was asleep. Then it went away. I heard some aeroplanes in the distance. It sounded like there were lots of them, and I wondered if they were Germans, coming to drop bombs. They went by though and the noise faded. I thought Mary must have gone too by now, so I opened my eyes.

She was still crouching there, looking right at me. I made a startled noise.

"I knew you was watching," she said.

"Watching what?" I said.

"You tell Mum and I'll kill you," she said. "Got it?"

I nodded.

Mary stood and put the tin back. Then she grabbed what she had taken, and went.

My heart was beating fast. I knew my mum kept a tin in a cupboard which had some savings in it.

Had Mary stolen some of her mum's money?

***

At last, one cool summer morning, a letter came for me. I could see it was Mr Florey's handwriting. My heart missed a beat, and I felt a sickness of excitement and fear in my throat. Part of me wanted to rip the letter open and start reading it right there and then, and part of me was terrified because of what news it might contain. I almost found myself regretting having asked Mr Florey to be honest with me about Ronny. Mrs Hill had an endless list of chores for me to do that day, and for the first time, I was pleased to have to do them as they kept my mind from worrying, and gave me an excuse to delay reading the letter. The morning grew hotter, and I worked harder than ever, trying to keep my mind busy. But, no matter how hard I tried, I found myself thinking about Ronny, and what Mr Florey might have to tell me.

All afternoon, as I swept the floor, and chopped the vegetables and put the peelings on the compost heap and changed the baby and got the coal in, I tried to imagine what might be in Mr Florey's letter. I had to force my dinner down. I could hardly eat, but I knew I would be hungry, and in trouble, if I didn't. After dinner, I had to do the dishes, and then sweep the floor again, and wash all the baby's nappies. That was a horrible job. I had to scrape all the mess off outside first, into the stinging nettles, then fill the wooden tub with hot water from the kettle, and scrub the nappies up and down the washboard for ages. The hot water, and the soap flakes, and the bumpy metal surface of the washboard all made my fingers sore. Afterwards, when I had put the nappies through the mangle, and hung them on the line in the garden, my hands were red and aching.

But at least I had a bit of time to read my letter now. Or so I thought.

Mrs Hill came down the stairs wearing her best dress, and lots of makeup. "Fill the kettle, Jill," she said. "I've got people coming."

So, while Mrs Hill and her friends sat and played cards round the kitchen table, I had to keep the kettle boiled and make them lots of cups of the stuff we called tea. I thought they would stay forever. They just kept on starting new games, and finding new things to talk about. One of the women was the billeting officer who had brought me here. I wished her and Mrs Hill weren't such good friends. Billeting officers were supposed to make sure we evacuees were happy and well looked after, but how could I tell one of Mrs Hill's best friends that I wasn't?

At last, I managed to creep out to the hall for a while, but it was too dark there to see Mr Florey's writing. I didn't have a lamp and there were no lights in Mrs Hill's house. So I decided to go outside to read it. It was still not properly dark yet.

I lifted the latch as quietly as I could. The door creaked as it opened, but laughter was coming from the kitchen. They didn't hear me. It was warmer outside than it was inside, and there was still a bit of daylight left in the sky. I pulled the door closed and sat in the grass by the front wall. I could see the air-raid warden a bit further up the street, out on her patrol. She was heading towards the town, so she didn't see me. Even though I was still fearful of what the letter might contain, I knew that I had to read it now, quickly, before Mrs Hill found me out. I slid the letter from my skirt pocket, nervously tore open the envelope, and began to read.

"Dear Jilly, again I must apologise to you. I have been dreadful at replying to your letters, and you deserve honesty from me. You are right, I have not been telling you everything." I realised my hands had begun to shake. I didn't want to read any more, but I couldn't stop myself. "I wish I could tell you that Ronny was becoming strong and healthy and no longer needs his medicine. I cannot tell you that, Jilly. He is growing though, and he is getting stronger. He is much bigger than when you last saw him, but he does still need the medicine every day. I think he always will. You see, it is very important for any young animal to have its mother's milk, which is full of goodness. Ronny didn't have that, which we think is why his body is not very good at fighting illness. Last month, he was very sick. He couldn't keep his food down, and I was very worried about him. I didn't want to tell you that though. But you will be pleased to know he is much better now. But I know what you are thinking. You are wondering if Doctor Barker will decide the medicine is too expensive. I have to tell you, Jilly, that the medicine does cost the zoo a lot of money, and with the war shortages getting worse, we might not be able to keep on affording it. It's not all bad though. You must be hopeful. We have managed to find people to adopt some of the zoo animals. That means that a shop or business or public club gives us money for that animal's food and upkeep. It is unlikely that anyone will be willing to adopt a poorly animal, but Ronny will still benefit because it means the zoo has a little more money to spare now, thanks to sponsors of other animals. And you must remember that Doctor Barker loves all animals, and ending their lives is always a last resort." I shook my head at that bit. Doctor Barker was my enemy, and Ronny's too. "For the time being, Ronny is safe, and is in no danger, just as before you went away. But rest assured that if that situation changes, I will write to you immediately so that you can come and say goodbye to him." I had one hand over my mouth by now. I was shaking my head and my eyes were full of tears. I blinked them away and carried on reading. "I have been honest with you at last, Jilly. I hope you can forgive me for keeping the truth from you. Please understand I was only trying to protect your feelings. I realise now though that I underestimated you. You are becoming a strong minded and brave young lady. I admire your directness. Please write again soon. Your friend..."

I don't know how long I sat there for. I didn't even notice Tim coming along the road.

"What you doing there?" he said, and I jumped. It was nearly dark by now. "Gave me a fright," he said. "I nearly walked right into you." I looked up at him, but couldn't speak. I wished he was Pete. "You alright?" he said. I looked away again. "Jill?" He crouched down. He was wearing his Wellingtons and denims. He'd been helping out at the farm. I could smell cigarettes on him too. "What's up? Mam upset you?" I shook my head. "Come on, 'course she has. What's she done now?"

"It's not your mum," I managed to say.

"You crying? You are aren't you. Come on, tell your uncle Timmy." He sat down next to me. "That a letter? Can I see?"

I don't know why, but I let him read it. It took him a while because the light was fading, and he wasn't familiar with Mr Florey's handwriting.

"So..." he said, when he'd finished. "There's a sick tiger is there? Shame. I like tigers myself."

"Do you?" I said.

"'Course I do. Who doesn't? Strong, mighty beasts of power, and handsome too. Much like my good self!" I managed to smile at that. "Tell me about..." He looked back at the letter, "Ronny."

So I told him. He really was interested. When I'd finished, he said, "Sad, that. Dead sad. I'll bet you wish you was back in London." I nodded. "Well, maybe you can do something to help him, even from here."

"Could I?"

"Well, like your friend said, some places will give money to feed the animals." I looked at him. "So, why don't you ask around? You never know what people might say."

I nodded.

"You're dead lucky though," he said. "I know he's sick an' all, but wow! A tiger! I'd love to be able to look after a tiger, sick or not."

Just then, there was the sound of ladies laughing and chattering behind me. Tim suddenly stood up. Mrs Hill was saying goodbye to her friends. One came down the path. I got up and brushed my skirt down. I put the letter in my pocket. The ladies walked by me and looked down at me. One of them smiled. One patted my head. The billeting officer who had brought me here just looked at me. She was as unfriendly now as Mrs Hill. I wondered what bad things Mrs Hill had told her about me. They walked off down the road, chatting.

Mrs Hill looked at me. "Get in," she said. I hurried inside leaving her and Tim out in the street. As I went, I heard her asking Tim where he'd been. He answered, but I couldn't tell what he said. I heard Mrs Hill yelling at him. I don't even know why. They came inside and she followed him up the stairs, yelling and stamping her feet. Then I heard him cry out.

I couldn't stop myself. I went out into the hall. "Leave him alone!" I called. Then I added, "Please."

I heard a door slam upstairs. Mrs Hill came down, slowly. She said, "*What* did you say?"

"Please," I said, "Tim hasn't done anything wrong. He was just talking to me, that's all."

"This ent got nothing to do with you, madam. I'll thank you to keep your nose out of my business. Now, there's some cups in there needs washing. Then you can get into bed, girl. And don't you ever pull a disappearing act like that on me ever again. If you were one o' mine, oh, I'd..." Then, shaking her head and hissing like a snake, she just pointed into the kitchen. I turned, half expecting her strike me round the back of the head, and I walked into the kitchen as calmly as I could. With shaking hands, I started to gather the cups and saucers from the table. Behind me, Mrs Hill slammed the kitchen door, nearly making me drop a cup, and it was only when I heard her footsteps on the stairs that I realised I was alone.

Chapter 13

I had a dream one night. My dad was there, walking with me through the zoo, holding my hand. He was talking to me in a deep, gentle voice, telling me I could help Ronny. "You can save him, my darling," he said, "if you really try. It won't be easy, but you must try." When I woke up, I felt as if Dad was still there, like a ghost, or an angel. And I remembered something Pete had once said. Something like, would I prefer never to have known Ronny, to save myself the worry and sadness of losing him? I knew I wouldn't. And I wished I could have known Dad too. I wished he had lived longer, been my dad for a while, before he died. I'd have preferred that.

Throughout the summer, I had to spend the whole time doing jobs for Mrs Hill. Some of the other children in the village helped out on the farm, or joined the Cogs. Cogs collected anything that could be salvaged, like wood and rubber and metal and paper, for the war effort. Some of my friends from school had joined, but I couldn't because Mrs Hill said I didn't have time. The only time I got a break was when she sent me to the shops to get the week's rations. At least I was out of the house. It was a hot summer. There were little swarms of flies in the air and they wouldn't leave you alone.

And I had a plan that would save my tiger.

The Butcher's shop had red stone tiles on the floor. Even though meat was rationed now, there always seemed to be lots of rabbits and ducks hanging in the window, and loads of sausages and pies on the display underneath. There was a bit of a queue that day. Excited, I waited my turn, then passed Mrs Hill's ration book up the butcher. He was a big man, with a very brown, rough looking face and little eyes. He was wearing his white hat and overalls, with a blue stripy apron on top.

"Mr Weatherby," I said. I knew his name because it was written on the sign outside. "I was wondering if I could ask you something." Mum always told me you are much more likely to get what you want if you are polite. I was excited, and couldn't hide my smile.

"Mmm?" he said as he chopped a string of sausages into bits, and weighed them. He didn't sound very interested. He didn't even look at me.

"Well..." I had planned out my speech in my head, but I had expected him to stop what he was doing. "There's a very beautiful tiger in London Zoo called Ronny."

"Want 'im made into sausages do you?"

"No!" I said, shocked. The lady behind me laughed, and I felt myself going red.

"Well, what you tellin' me about it for then?"

"Well..."

"Spit it out, lass, I 'aven't got all day."

I'd forgotten my speech now, but I was doing this for Ronny. I wouldn't give up. "This tiger, he's sick and he needs lots of medicine."

Mr Weatherby was throwing the meat into paper bags and spinning them over to twist them closed. "I ent a veterinary," he said, and I saw him glancing at the lady behind. I looked at her. She was pretty. I think she was the mum of someone in my school. She was smiling at Mr Weatherby.

I carried on. "His medicine costs lots of money, but the zoo hasn't got much money because of the war. If they can't afford his medicine—"

"One and thruppence."

"Er... well, that's very kind, thank you. Every little bit will help, but—"

"For the sausages. One and thruppence. It's what you owe me."

I couldn't believe he'd just interrupted me like

that. The lady behind me sniggered. Feeling stupid, I got the money out of my pocket and handed it to him. He turned his back on me then, and I heard the till opening and closing. He handed me my change.

"Thank you," I said. Mr Weatherby was looking down at me. I decided to try once more, now that I had his attention. "But this tiger, they might have to..." I could hardly bring myself to say the word, "...to kill it, because of the money."

"Money?"

"Yes, for his medicine."

"And... *then* you want me to make him into sausages?"

"No!" I went red again. I heard the lady trying not to laugh.

"Well, what then?"

"Well, he needs money, see. I'm trying to find someone who will adopt him, so that—"

"Adopt him? Where would I put him?"

"No," I said, not sure if he was making fun of me. "It means you give the zoo money, to buy his food and medicine."

"What's in it for me?"

"Well..." I realised I didn't know that. I had just thought people would *want* to help save a tiger's life.

Surprisingly, the lady helped me out then. "Maybe the zoo puts an advert up on his cage, to tell people about your shop." She smiled at me, and I nodded. Maybe that was the sort of thing that would interest Mr Weatherby.

"What, in London Zoo? Who's gonna come all the way out here from London? I know my sausages are good, but with the petrol shortage an' all... Sorry love, I've got too many other things to spend my money on." I stood there, knowing I should be able to find something else to say, knowing I would be letting Ronny down if I just walked away, but the lady cleared her throat, and tried to reach past me with her ration book. I moved aside. I knew I had failed. I took Mrs Hill's sausages, and left the shop.

I walked up the street to the baker's shop. I loved the baker's shop. The smells made me feel so hungry, but the shelves never had much on them. The baker was an old lady called Miss Bloome. She was a lot more friendly than Mr Weatherby. She seemed like someone who would love a tiger. I waited my turn, then told her about Ronny. She listened as I spoke, and she smiled all the time, and said things like, "Oooh lovely," and "how sad."

But at the end she said, "I'm so sorry I can't help you, dear. But good luck." And she started serving the next person.

All I could think of was poor Ronny wondering why I had left him.

Mr Jones the grocer wasn't interested either. I was embarrassed and angry, and I had failed Ronny. How could I ever look him in the eye again?

On the way home, George and Joe came running past with their friends, playing war. They shouted things at me. Sometimes they even did that in the house now too, and Mrs Hill didn't try to stop them. They called me 'stuck up,' and 'posh.' I tried to ignore them. Sometimes I thought they would never leave me alone. That day they walked behind me calling me 'posh nosh' the whole time. But just before I got home, Tim came along. He was on his way home from the Post Office for lunch.

"Oi," he said to Joe and George. They tried to run away, but he grabbed them by the hair. I stopped. "You being 'orrible to Jill?" he said.

"No!" they both said. Their faces were all screwed up and they kept whimpering.

"Don't lie."

"They were just being silly," I said. "It's alright though, I was ignoring them."

Tim suddenly yanked their hair and banged their heads together. It made me flinch. It must have really hurt. They both started to cry. He let them go and they ran off down the road. Tim shouted, "I'll do it twice as hard if I find you being horrible again!" I didn't know what to say. I didn't want him to hurt the twins, but I felt they deserved it too. I said, "Thanks," and he helped me carry the shopping bags home.

I told him about Mr Weatherby, and the other shop keepers. Tim nodded and frowned. Then he said, "You should try posters. You know, like the ones the government puts up. Like that one." He nodded towards the poster on the end wall of a house. It was a warning about keeping the blackout curtains closed tight. There was another one across the road with a big picture of a garden fork digging up a carrot, and the words 'Dig for victory'. "They catch people's eye, you know," Tim said. I nodded. Then I said, "But I haven't got any paper and paint." We were just arriving at the front gate.

"Well..." he said. "Dunno about paper, but I got some paints you can use. More for painting model planes, but they might work for a poster. Dunno about paper, though. Not much spare paper around these days. The Cogs have collected it all." I nodded. "Tell you what, I got an old bit of board I was going to use for something, but I've had it ages. I'll never use it. You could have that instead of paper."

"Thanks," I said, excited again now.

"No problem."

And I was already planning out my poster in my head.

***

It took me another week or so to get my poster finished. It was all I could think about, but I hardly ever had time to do it. Whenever I could get away, I went to the alleyway at the end of the garden, because I knew Mrs Hill wouldn't want me painting in the house. I couldn't do it when it rained, and it did seem to be raining quite a lot. And I couldn't do it when I had chores to do, which was nearly all the time. But at last, crouching in the gravel of the alleyway, between big bushes of stinging nettles and brambles, I finished it.

Tim only had black, green and white paint, so to make Ronny's orange stripes I had torn up a brown paper bag from the shop, and stuck strips of it onto the picture. The paint smelt funny, but it worked quite well as glue. I had painted Ronny looking as sad and lonely as possible, because I needed people to feel sorry for him, but it made me feel terrible to think of him like that. Above him, I had put 'Please help me. I don't want to die'. I had tried to think of a shorter sentence, or a rhyme, like on the war posters around the village. Most of them only had a few words on, and our teacher had told us that was to get the message across as quickly as possible. But there was so much I wanted to say about Ronny. At the bottom of the poster, I had put 'Together, we can save him'. I thought that was a good idea, because everyone was talking about working together, to support the war effort. I'd had to squash the words 'save him' up quite a lot to fit them on the board, and it didn't look as neat as I had wanted it to be. But people would be able to read it still, and how could they not want to help him then?

I didn't want to ruin Tim's brushes, so I scooped out some rain water from the barrel outside, and washed them as well as I could.

Once the poster had dried, I took it to the Post Office. Tim wasn't there that day, but Mr Jones, the owner, was. He was kind, and really fat but with twinkly eyes and a funny high voice. He had said I could stand my poster on top of the counter. He had an old shoe box, and he cut a slit in the top of it for me. "So folks can make their donations," he explained.

"If anyone says they want to adopt him, will you tell me?" I said.

"Of course. Or I'll get Tim to."

He gave me a ha'penny chew for free and patted my head.

If only everyone could be as nice as Mr Jones.

Chapter 14

It was the longest, loneliest summer of my life. Every night I lay awake in fear, hating the darkness of the blackout. Every morning, my shoulders, back and hips hurt from sleeping on the hard kitchen floor. And my fear for Ronny and sorrow for Pete stayed with me all day, every day. Mrs Hill always found more chores for me to do, and all I could think about was finding someone to adopt Ronny. After a while, I had asked at every shop in the town. A few people had given me money, but it was only a handful of coins, and no-one was willing to actually adopt him. There was never much money in the collection box at the Post Office, just a couple of coins every week. Still, I collected them and kept them hidden in my case.

I felt like a useless prisoner. I must have been the only person in the town not helping the war effort, and I certainly wasn't helping Ronny. Joe and George had joined the Cogs now. They often came home with a cart full of old metal pans and cans, and scruffy piles of torn up paper from people's bins. I thought they wouldn't want to help, but they seemed to love it. When Tim wasn't working in the Post Office, he spent quite a lot of time digging the vegetables in the garden, or working up at the farm with Mary.

Even Mrs Hill had joined a group of women in the village who helped organise the collecting and salvaging. They had set up a salvage dump at the edge of the town, and they sorted everything out into piles, so that the metal could be sent off to be made into guns and planes and tanks, and the silk could be made into parachutes and barrage balloons, and so on. They even collected books to send out for the soldiers to read, and they knitted socks and things for them too. At least she was out of the house a lot of the time now, but that just meant there was more work for me to do. I even had to mend all the boys' clothes and tidy their room up.

Mum visited again twice during the summer but I knew she wouldn't take me home with her. I'd seen the posters around town. They showed a mum and child sitting under a tree, and a ghost of Mr Hitler whispering in the mum's ear, trying to get her to take her daughter back to the city. They'd talked to us about it in school. They'd told us that we must stay with our billeters, for our own safety, no matter how much we wanted to go home.

So I stayed.

I used to wonder what Ronny was like now. It was so long since I'd seen him. Would he still remember me? Mr Florey wrote to me several more times that summer. Every time I got one of his letters I was terrified it was going to contain the news I dreaded. But he just told me how big Ronny was growing. It broke my heart to think of him growing up without me. Once, Mr Florey wrote that the wolf-man, Mr Kendal, had been up for a visit. "Every time he pops up, he has to come and see the great cats," the letter said. "He always asks about you, Jilly, and your mum. It seems you made quite an impression. I think he may invite the two of you down to see his menagerie, when he gets back from touring the country with his animal show. I imagine you'd like that very much."

I wondered about that. Perhaps it would be interesting to see Mr Kendal's animals.

And then I had an idea.

I needed writing paper, and I had run out. There was no spare paper anywhere at the moment. It had all been collected up by the Cogs to be turned into leaflets and posters. But I managed to find a corned beef tin that still had a label on, so I carefully removed it and used that. I wrote a letter to Mr Kendal. I had to use an old envelope from one of my mum's letters. I crossed out the address and peeled the stamp off. I didn't know Mr Kendal's address, but I sent it to Mr Florey, and wrote on the envelope 'Please forward to Mr Kendal (the wolf-man)'. Mr Florey had said Mr Kendal was away at the moment. I didn't know how long he'd be away for, and when, if ever, he would get my letter. But it was worth a try.

***

The summer didn't feel like a holiday. I was glad when school started again.

Shortly after that, I remember one horrible evening meal time, very clearly.

I finished laying the table for dinner and Mrs Hill called everyone in. The whole family was there, ready to eat. The baby was asleep in the front room though. We had made a big pie, and there were lots of vegetables from the garden, to go with it. I sat on my stool. Mrs Hill looked at me. She said, "No, I don't think so, love."

I didn't know what she meant. I looked around to see what I had done wrong. "No, love. I'll have just the family eating first today. You don't always seem to quite know how to dish yourself up a fair portion, and I've got my boys to think about."

I still didn't know what she meant.

"Get off the stool, dear," she said, very slowly. "You'll eat later. I'll make sure they leave you something." I felt my face burning up.

"Mum," Tim said, objecting.

"Don't you dare argue with me," Mrs Hill snapped. "I've got a family to feed, and the allowance we get for having 'er don't nearly cover what she eats." I wanted to hide my face. I wasn't greedy. In fact, I didn't eat much at all. But I didn't dare argue. "I won't have my family suffering because of *'er*."

"That's not fair, Mum," Mary said. "You can't do that." I was standing next to my stool now.

"I can do what I bloody well like. It's my house. Now eat yer dinner."

Mary stared at her, then pushed her plate away. "She can have mine," she said. She got up and went out of the house. I had never expected Mary to stick up for me.

Mrs Hill looked at me. For once the twins weren't laughing or messing around. Tim didn't say anything either. "Now look what you've done," she said. "Well, all the more for my boys." She started sharing Mary's dinner out onto their plates. I could feel my tummy rumbling. The food smelt really good, but I wouldn't have been able to eat now anyway. I wanted to run away, or just disappear, right there and then. I could feel them all looking at me, hating me, and thinking I was greedy. Mrs Hill told me to stand in the corner. I could feel a huge lump in my throat, but I wasn't going to let that woman see me cry.

I had to watch them all eating their dinner. Tim didn't look at me the whole time. Mrs Hill tried to make a conversation, but no-one wanted to talk.

When they'd finished, the twins left the kitchen and the house shook as they thundered up the stairs to their room. Tim still didn't look at me, but he looked at his mum, as if he wanted to say something. But she had her back to him, putting the tiny bit of pie that was left onto a plate for me. Then she scraped the boy's plates onto it too. I wanted to stop her. What was she doing? Did she expect me to eat that? I thought Tim was going to say something. Maybe together we could get her to stop being so horrible, to all of us.

But he didn't say anything. He just went.

And I was on my own.

I had to clear the table and wash the dishes,

even though I still hadn't eaten anything. When I'd put everything away, she said I could sit down and eat my pie.

It looked horrible. I didn't want to eat what she'd scraped off the boys' plates. It was cold too. I said I didn't feel well.

"What? Is my family's food not good enough for you? Mm?"

"I'm just not very hungry," I said. It was true. I wasn't anymore. I felt too sick to eat anything. I desperately wanted my mum, and Pete and Ronny.

"Well, you insult me," she said. "You'll just have to go without." And she tipped it into the rubbish bucket. "There's a war on, you know. It's a sin to waste such good food in times like these."

***

I wanted to thank Mary for sticking up for me, but it was hard. She wasn't easy to talk to, and I was very nervous around her. But, the next day, when Mrs Hill was talking to a neighbour in the street, Mary came into the kitchen for something, and I quickly blurted out, "Thank you… for yesterday. For… trying to…"

But she just said, "Any nappies ready?" It was

as if she didn't want me to thank her. I dug one out of the clean pile and handed it to her. She gave a quick smile and turned to go. But she stopped in the doorway and said, "You'll have to toughen up, girl. Sometimes you got to stick up for yourself." And then she disappeared into the front room where the baby had begun to cry.

Every meal time was the same now. Mrs Hill didn't let me eat with them anymore, and all she gave me were the leftovers. Just looking at what she scraped off their plates made me feel sick, even though I was starving most of the time. Mary didn't object any more, although she often wasn't there for meals anyway. Maybe Mary expected me to stick up for myself now, like she'd said. But I just couldn't talk to Mrs Hill the way she had.

Mrs Hill made me do more jobs than ever after that. I kept falling asleep in school. My teacher asked me if everything was alright. I was worried she would come and talk to Mrs Hill, like Mum had, and make everything even worse for me. Or maybe she'd even talk to the billeting officer, but the billeting officer was Mrs Hill's friend, so I told her I was fine. I told her I couldn't sleep because I was so upset about my brother. That was partly true, but afterwards, I felt sick with guilt for telling a lie about Pete.

But one day I heard something that made me really scared for Mum and for Ronny. I had gone to the Post Office to get some stamps for Mrs Hill. I was waiting in the queue, and there was an old lady in front of me. She was reading a newspaper. Tim wasn't working there today, but the old lady was talking to Mr Jones. "It's terrible, Ern," she said. I think Mr Jones's name was Ernie. He nodded and his big face wobbled about like a jelly. "I just can't bear to think about what could happen. Do you think Mr Churchill will see them off? There's only the Channel between us and the Germans. Less than that even, they've taken the Channel Isles." Mr Jones nodded again, and looked very concerned. Then he looked at me and winked. But the old lady was in my way, so I couldn't get to the counter. "I never thought I'd see the day. We're sitting ducks here, you know. And now they're bombing our air fields and factories... Where will it end? Where will it end?"

I got my stamps, and started to walk home. Half way home I saw Joe and George. They were standing on the wall at the edge of a field. There were other children there too. They were looking at the sky. In the distance, it was full of long, curly white lines, like pieces of thread. There were not very many clouds so we could see them clearly. I didn't know what they were at first. Some of the land girls working in the field had stopped to look too. Some of the boys went running across the field. There was a very faint hum. It was planes, flying about in circles, soaring high and diving like pigeons playing. Lots of the children were shouting and cheering, yelling things like, "Come on, kill the Gerry!" The planes were just tiny dots from here, and I wouldn't have known which planes were ours and which were German even if I could see them properly. There was a sudden spark of light in the sky, coming from one of them. Then it began to dive, and instead of leaving a white line, now it left a grey one as it plummeted straight towards the ground. A few moments later, there was another burst of light as the plane crashed, far off, beyond the trees. The smoke rising from it was thick and dark on the horizon. Some of the children cheered.

Just then, Mrs Hill shouted down the road at me, "Jill! Where are you, for God's sake? I told you to come straight back!" She came marching towards me in her housecoat and slippers. She was holding her feather duster. I ran over to her. "Sorry," I said. "But there's..."

"Get in," she said, and then she did something she'd not done to me before. She hit me. It hurt and I nearly fell over. I yelled, and clutched my ear. I think Mrs Hill was looking around to see if anyone had seen what she'd done. I had dropped the little bag of stamps. "Pick it up," she said, and walked away. I did as she said. My ear was stinging. With tears hurting my eyes, I followed her back to the house.

When we got to the kitchen, she made me sit down at the table. She said, "I been hearing things, girl. I been hearing things about you in the village. Is it true?"

I didn't know what she was talking about. She leaned on the table and glared at me. Her face was bright red. Then she thumped the table, making me jump. "You been going round the shops beggin'? Well?"

I shook my head and tried to speak, but couldn't make any sound come out. "What is it, then? I don't provide for you? Mm? It ent my fault I got a family to feed and not enough money to do it, is it?" I shook my head. "You want people to think I ent looking after you good enough? Because that's what they think!" She was nearly screaming. I had never seen someone in such a rage before. I was terrified she was going to hit me again. "Stop cowering, you little madam," she yelled. I tried to, but it was hard. She was standing really close to me. "I tell you, if I hear any more stories about you going begging, I don't know what I'll do, God help me." She stared at me, and then she just turned and left, slamming the kitchen door behind her.

I cried. Partly because I was so scared, partly because my ear hurt, but mostly because I was so angry. How dare she tell me I couldn't help Ronny anymore? There was no way I was going to just put up with that.

Chapter 15

That night, I decided to tell Mum everything. I knew that could make Mrs Hill even worse when she found out, but maybe Mum would come and take me back to London. Or maybe she'd arrange for me to stay with a different family. That was something that hadn't occurred to me before, but I'd found out in school that one of the children in the village had been moved to a different family because their billeter hadn't wanted them. I'd never realised you could do that. I'd always assumed it was Mrs Hill or nothing. I think Mum must have done too.

I waited until everyone had gone to bed, and I couldn't hear the boys playing in their room any more. Then I got a little oil lamp down, poured some oil in, and lit it with a match. I made sure the blackout curtains were drawn properly. It was just bright enough for me to see by, but I'd have to blow it out if I heard any footsteps on the stairs. I had some paper and a pencil which Mum had given me, so I sat on my bed, under the table, with my back against the wall, and wrote my letter. It was really hard to write because I didn't have anything to rest on, and the light flickered a lot in the draft from the door. I wished I could sit at the table to write, but I wouldn't have had time to hide the letter and put the lamp out if I heard anyone coming. I began to cry as I wrote, because I knew how bad Mum would feel when she read it. I almost forgot to mention that the billeting officer was Mrs Hill's friend! I just hoped Mum would let me come straight back to London.

I posted my letter the next day.

And then I waited.

Day after day, I listened for the post man, frightened and excited, and trying to act normally in front of Mrs Hill.

But after two whole weeks I had still not had a reply. I was worried about Mum. What if something had happened? It was not until one Sunday, in church, that I found out about the air-raids.

"Let us pray," the vicar said, "for those poor victims of German viciousness and hatred. I'm talking of course about the innocent, noble and brave inhabitants of our King's city, where this week a great many bombs have been falling."

My heart stopped.

My stomach tore in half.

Was that why Mum had not written to me?

I wanted to run out of the church screaming. I wanted to get on the next train and go home to her.

And then I had another horrible thought. What if the bombs got Ronny? Just because he wasn't a person didn't mean he was safe from the bombs. He would be all alone and afraid. He would want me to be comforting him. I had failed to raise money for his medicine, or to find someone to adopt him. Now I had to go to him!

I couldn't listen to another word the vicar said. I felt as if I wasn't there in the church at all. It seemed like forever before the service ended and we got up to leave. Even then, as always, Mrs Hill spent ages talking to the other mums, while Joe and George ran around making lots of noise and bumping into people. Tim waited until Mrs Hill wasn't looking, and he quietly went over to a pretty girl who was in his year at our school. I saw them laughing together while her parents talked to the vicar about something. Mary hadn't come to the church with us, so now there was no-one watching me. I didn't want to just walk away from Tim. He'd been kind to me at times, and I wanted to thank him. But it was impossible. I had to go now.

I couldn't believe what I was about to do. But I

couldn't believe what had already happened either. Everything was so bad, I *had* to do it. I walked away, out of the church, into the sunshine. I sped up, and then I started to run. I ran all the way back to the house, as fast as I could, because if Mrs Hill caught me she'd have beaten me worse than ever. The front door was never locked, and I ran straight up to the boys' room where all my clothes and my case were.

The room smelt horrible, as always, and was so messy I didn't know where to walk. There was bedding and clothes and toys, and bits of broken wood and old bricks and oily machines and model aeroplanes all over the place. I made my way over to the drawers. My heart was beating really fast. If they came back now, I'd be in such trouble.

I pulled my clothes out of the drawer and threw them into my case. There was a pocket in the lid of my case where I kept all my money and the little things Mum sent me. I reached in and...

It was gone.

I kept feeling around inside the pocket. How could it not be there? I checked through my case, to see if it had fallen out of the pocket, but I couldn't find it. I wanted to scream. How was I going to pay for my train ticket now? And it wasn't just that.

The few coins I'd collected for Ronny were gone, too. I pulled all my clothes out onto the filthy floor, and searched through everything, listening for the sound of the door all the time. My money, and my presents, had all gone.

I stood up. Surely those boys...

They were badly behaved, and they were sometimes horrible to me, but they wouldn't steal my money, would they?

Then I saw it. The little wooden tiger Mum had sent me. It was on the floor between the mattresses. I stared at it. They *had* stolen my things. I almost yelled in anger. Instead, I took some deep breaths, then picked it up and put it in my skirt pocket. I wanted to find everything of mine, but there wasn't time. What I needed most was my money. I was sure I would hear the door opening, and Mrs Hill shouting at me any minute. I started searching through the mess, being careful to put it all back as it was. But I knew I wouldn't find my money. There was no time, and it probably wasn't even there. I wondered if I'd be able to get on the train without a ticket. I wondered if I could just walk back home. Then... I remembered something.

I threw everything back into my case. I couldn't

fasten up the buckles though. I remembered Mum having to sit on it when she closed it for me before I came here. I tried that, but I wasn't strong enough. My heart was racing. I was sweating too, and breathing fast. I'd never felt so scared.

I decided to leave my case.

I ran downstairs to the kitchen. I pulled the stool over to the side and climbed up, kneeling on it. There were lots of tins on the top shelf. I shook each one. At last I found one which jangled. I got down and put it on the table. I pulled the lid off. There were several pound notes in it, and lots of coins. I glanced behind me at the front door. I didn't know if Mrs Hill was coming up the garden path, or if she was still minutes away. I hoped she was still at the church.

I took a handful of money. I counted it quickly. I knew how much Mum had given me, and there was a lot more than that here. But I only took what they owed me. I put the rest back in the tin.

But then Mary came out of the front room holding the baby. I was so surprised I dropped the tin. It clashed against the floor and the coins spilled out and rolled everywhere. I hadn't even realised she was in the house.

"Wha' do you think you're doing?" she said. I

didn't speak. She came towards me. "What are you..."

Behind Mary, the front door flew open and the twins charged up the stairs. Mrs Hill must still have been a bit further away because I couldn't see her yet.

"You nicking from us now?" Mary said. She jigged her baby up and down.

"I only took what was mine."

"What's in that tin ent yours."

"It isn't yours either," I said.

Mary sighed. "Well, Little Miss Goody Two Shoes, I never took you for a thief. You're as bad as me now. Take the money." I stared at her. "Go on," she said. Confused, my heart thumping, I quickly stuffed the money I was holding into my dress pocket. "Pick the rest up, there's a good girl." Mary watched as I frantically gathered up all the coins I could, shoved them into the tin, and put the tin back on the shelf. She looked at me for a while, with a strange grin on her face, and then she gave a little laugh as if she was very pleased with herself. I still didn't understand. Was she helping me? Then I realised. She probably didn't know the boys had taken my money. She just thought I was a thief. And she didn't know I was running away.

She knew Mrs Hill would be here any second, and she thought she'd be able to get her to find the money in my pockets. Then Mary would always be able to take what she wanted from the tin, and I'd get the blame every time. She looked at me as she walked round the table. I thought she was going to try to get me to change the baby, or feed him. But she just picked up the box of matches. Then she went back into her room.

I could hear Mrs Hill and Tim's voices at the front door. There was only one thing I could do.

I went out of the back door. I ran down the garden, the nettles stinging my bare legs. I scrambled past the Anderson shelter, and pulled the gate open.

And I was in the back alley.

I ran all the way round until I came out into the street. There were still some people there coming back from church. I walked when I went past them. I didn't want them to know I was running away. But I was sure Mrs Hill would soon be coming up behind me. When I was past them all, I started to run again. I was hot, but the drizzle in the air cooled me down. There were more people further ahead, but I climbed over a wall and cut across the field, past the stripy cows. There was a little bit of woodland before the station and it took me a while to get through the brambles and fallen trees. I came out by the main road. I slid down the bank. I was filthy now, and I'd cut my legs. I hurried along the road towards the station. When I got there, my hair and clothes were wet from the rain. I didn't care though. I was excited to be going home, to see Mum and Ronny. But I was scared, too, that something dreadful had happened to them.

I was the only one in the station. When I went to buy my ticket, the lady looked at me over her spectacles and said, "Are you sure?"

I nodded, and offered her the money.

"You know, the government says you shouldn't travel if you don't have to." She waved her hand at a poster on the wall.

"I know, but... My mum says I have to go home."

"Well, if your mum says... But must you really go into London, of all places?"

I nodded. I was worried she wasn't going to give me the ticket.

"I don't know," she said. She looked at me without speaking for a while. I shuffled my feet. "Aren't you the tiger-girl?" she said. I nodded. "I remember you. I was in the fishmongers when you came in and asked for money. You really going to give that money to the zoo?"

"Yes," I said, although I remembered, with dismay, that I didn't even have that money any more. I wished the lady would stop asking questions and let me have the ticket.

"I been to the zoo once. Saw the tigers. Lovely creatures," she said. "Tell you what, if I give you the ticket half-price, will you give the other half to the zoo?"

"Oh, yes!" I said, smiling suddenly.

"Alright. But you look after yourself in London, my dear. Tell your mum to take you somewhere safe."

"I will," I said. "Thank you very much!"

I got my ticket, and sat on the bench in the waiting room. The big clock ticked loudly. I would have to wait more than an hour for the train. I was terrified Mrs Hill would come in and try to drag me back. I wouldn't go this time though. I'd run away from her if I had to. I'd even fight her. I never wanted to be in that house ever again. I felt bad about Mary though. She'd stuck up for me once, and now she thought I was stealing from them. She wasn't particularly nice, but it was horrible to think I'd let her down so badly. If only I'd had time to explain. Suddenly, I thought the police might be looking for me because I'd stolen the money. I kept watching the door, but no-one came in. Perhaps, because I'd left my case behind, no-one would realise I'd gone to the station. They'd think I was coming back, but I wasn't. I had brought nothing with me, not even my tiger teddy. I wished I had thought to bring it, I wanted to hold him and press my face into his fur. But I did have my little wooden tiger in my pocket. I clutched it tight, and wished for Pete.

At half past one, the train arrived. I took one last look behind me and climbed on board. I could have cried with relief. I found an empty carriage and sat down.

I was going home.

Chapter 16

King's Cross station was full of smoke and steam and noise, as usual. I already felt as if I had come home. Pigeons swooped and dived and train whistles shrieked. I was hungry, and a lady was selling apples, so I bought one.

I walked up the street towards Camden, eating my apple. It felt comforting to be surrounded by tall houses again, and to see so many lorries, cars and carts. A trolleybus went by, making sparks where it touched the overhead wires, and a band was playing somewhere. The barrage balloons swayed above the city like fish above a river bed.

I jumped on a bus outside the station, and went up onto the top deck. I stared out of the window as it wound its way up towards Camden. Everyone in the street was carrying their gas masks. I had forgotten mine. The conductor said I shouldn't be out without a gas mask. "Never know what they're going to drop next time," he said. I smiled, and paid for my ticket, but his warning scared me.

As we waited at a bus stop, I noticed the next street up was closed off with wooden barriers. The bus pulled away, and as we passed the end of the street, I saw something that made me stop chewing my apple, and stare. Half way down, there was a big gap in the row of tall terraced houses. Where the house should have been, there was a massive pile of rubble that went right across the road. There were men and women digging in it. Even inside the bus, I could taste the dust in the air.

Suddenly I felt sicker than ever. Had this happened to our flat too?

I had to change busses when I got to Camden High Street.

On the second part of my journey I saw more closed roads and ruined buildings. The whole place smelled of brick-dust and smoke. One entire street was filled with rubble, only a few broken walls still standing. On the main street, many of the buildings had smashed windows, and debris on the road had been swept into big piles. One building had no front, and you could see into all the rooms. The rubble was blocking some of the road, and barriers had been put around it. There were children clambering on the rubble, and a woman shouting at them to get down.

At my last stop, I jumped off the bus before it had even properly stopped, and ran to Princess Terrace.

To my relief, our row was all still there. So Mum must be alright! I ran up the steps. I suddenly realised I didn't have my key, so I banged on the door, and waited. Mum didn't answer, but I knew she always kept a spare under the mat, so I pulled it out. I went in and shouted, "Mum! Mum!" I ran into the kitchen. She wasn't there. I ran into the sitting room. Then into her bedroom, and my bedroom. It was pointless. Mum wasn't anywhere in the flat. I suddenly thought, maybe there had been a bomb at her work, or when she was just walking along the street. My stomach hurt with worry again. I was desperate to go to see Ronny, but I wouldn't do anything until I knew about my mum. I sat down at the table in the kitchen. I couldn't think of anything to do except wait. I must have been exhausted because I put my head on my arms, and fell asleep.

When I woke up, Mum still wasn't there. I checked round the whole flat again just in case. I was starving. I found some cold meat and bread and cheese. I ate, then I washed up my plate and knife. I decided I would go to the zoo. Maybe Mum would get back while I was out. I was worried she'd be cross with me for running away. I was worried the police had told her I'd stolen the money. But I was more worried something terrible had happened to her.

I went out into the street. It only took me a few minutes to walk up to the zoo. There was a young girl who I didn't know in the ticket office. At first, she wouldn't let me in without paying, and I didn't have enough money left to buy a ticket. I told her about Mr Florey, and said I was going to see him. She didn't know who he was, but it was only a few minutes until the zoo would be closing, so she said it couldn't do any harm, and she let me in.

I felt excited to be there. It was raining a little bit, but the sun was shining on the trees at the same time, and the air seemed to glow. I went straight to the Lion House, even though I wanted to stop and look at the camels, and the elephants, and all the other animals I hadn't seen for such a long time. My heart was beating fast. I was scared for so many different reasons. Would Ronny recognise me? Would he forgive me for going away from him? Would he even be there at all?

I went round the outside first. I saw the lions and lionesses, and the cheetah and the other tigers. The giant panda was scratching his tummy and chewing some bamboo. I loved all the animals, but Ronny was *my* tiger. I went inside. There was his enclosure.

My heart stopped.

There was a fully grown tiger in there, and no sign of Ronny. What had they done with him?

Then I realised, this was Ronny. Even though Mr Florey had told me how big he was, I was still expecting him to look like a cub.

I called his name. I didn't care if the other visitors thought I was a bit strange. He looked up at me. He looked right into my eyes. In that moment, I was suddenly reminded of the time Ronny the First had looked into my eyes on that dreadful day at the start of the war. Then, he came over to where I was standing and I leaned against the barrier. "I love you so much," I said to him. He made a little growling noise. It was a gentle noise, but it was so deep, it surprised me. Did he forgive me for leaving him? A little boy and his mum were looking at me. I smiled at them.

Then... I nearly screamed. Ronny had been sick! I'd thought he was much more healthy now, but... Mr Florey had promised to be honest with me, but he hadn't said Ronny was getting sick again...

I was nearly sick too. Some of the visitors had noticed, and were peering at it. There was nothing else I could do. I had to go in and be close to him.

I went out and round to the keeper's entrance. I opened the door. "Mr Florey," I called as I went inside. "It's me, Jill!"

I heard footsteps on the stairs. A young man, chubby and with orange hair, came down, into the corridor. He had spots, like Tim's, and was younger than Pete.

"Who are you?" he said. He sniffed. "You can't come in here."

"My name's Jill," I said. "Mr Florey lets me come in."

"Mr Florey ent here," he said.

I said, "Oh." I just stood there.

"Well, could you go please?" the man said.

"Can I wait for Mr Florey?"

"No. He ent coming back tonight. Zoo's closing in a minute."

"Well, can I please wait, and go in with my tiger when everyone's gone?"

"What? *Your* tiger!" He laughed. "Off you go love."

"Ronny. He's my tiger. Well, he's not really mine, but I look after him. I've been away and..."

"Ronny? Oh, the young'un? I wouldn't get too attached to him, love. Mr Florey said he ent going to be here much longer."

"What? No!"

"Yer. Doctor Barker said his medicine costs too much. Shame. I quite liked him myself."

I turned and ran outside. It was raining hard now. I put my hand over my mouth to stop me screaming.

I felt dizzy. Someone asked if I was alright, but I just walked past them. I didn't go to see Ronny again. I couldn't look into his eyes knowing they were going to kill him.

I wouldn't let it happen. I didn't know how to stop it, but somehow, I would.

Chapter 17

I don't even remember walking home. But I had just turned down my street when I saw something that got me out of my trance. A policeman was just going up the steps to my front door. I stopped.

I'd only stolen the money because they'd stolen mine! Maybe I should just go and tell him that. But if he put me in prison, how could I help Ronny? I crouched down behind a pillar box. The policeman kept knocking on the door. He stood there for ages. He shouted something through the letterbox. He knocked again. Then he went back down the steps and walked away.

When he'd gone, I ran to my door and quickly let myself in.

I went round the whole flat again looking for Mum. She'd have answered the door to the policeman if she was in, but I tried every room anyway. I cried. It was getting dark, and I fell asleep at the kitchen table again.

Later, I went to my bed. It was so long since I'd slept in my bed. Even though I was feeling terrible about everything, my soft bed felt beautiful. I slept straight away.

But later, a loud noise woke me up. At first, I thought I was back in Mrs Hill's house, and the baby was crying. I tried to make myself wake up. The wailing noise slowly trailed away and stopped, but I realised what it was. We'd had lots of air-raid practices in school, so I recognised the sound of the siren. But it was quiet now, and I still felt half asleep. I wondered if I'd dreamed it. I didn't want to open my eyes, but when I did I suddenly remembered I was alone. The darkness felt cold and frightening, and I sat up on my bed, listening. My heart was racing. I felt as if I was drowning in the darkness of the blackout.

I told myself not to be so stupid. I never used to be scared of the dark. I wanted to go back to sleep, but I rubbed my eyes instead, to wake myself up.

I couldn't hear any planes or bombs yet. Maybe it was a false alarm. We'd had one of those on the first day of the war. But I'd seen the bombed houses today. And then I began to hear the bombs for real. It took me a few seconds to realise. The noise was odd, like a distant moan, not the bang I had expected. But I heard the whistling too, and the moans got louder and clearer and sharper. The bombs were getting closer.

I knew I had to go to the Morrison shelter in the

kitchen. I got dressed, trying not to panic. The bombs got even louder, and sounded more like thunder now. It made the floor shake. I put my shoes on and ran to the kitchen.

Someone was standing there, and my heart nearly burst with shock.

I couldn't see who it was because it was so dark. For a second, I thought it might be Mum. But I could hear horrible, hissing breathing, and their body was bent. Then there was a flash of light as an explosion shook the building, and I saw the face. It wasn't human. It was lumpy and shiny and its lips were twisted and horrible, and it had no hair on one side of its head and it was coming towards me. It made a terrifying noise, like a wireless not tuned in, and reached out at me...

I don't even know if I screamed. My mind went blank. I just ran out of the flat. The bombs shook the ground so hard they nearly made me fall over. I could smell dust and smoke. Booming noises hurt my ears. I couldn't think. I ran up the street. Someone shouted at me, "Get inside!" It was an A.R.P. officer. He blew his whistle and shouted again but I kept running. I only wanted Ronny. A man and a woman were running from the pub at the end of the road. "Get that light off!" the A.R.P.

officer yelled.

I ran until I could hardly breathe. Didn't know if any of those people were chasing me, if the *thing* was chasing me. Past the church and over Prince Albert Road without even looking. Couldn't go into the zoo, it was all locked up. Instead, I ran past it, along Prince Albert Road. Didn't know why. Over the canal and then I realised I was running on the grass of Regent's Park, right beside the zoo.

I stopped. Behind me, the sky was red. The bombs were still falling, whistling like kettles as they rained down, each explosion making an earthquake. I could hear the planes too, filling the air with their deathly drone. Hardly thinking, I walked along beside the zoo wall. I knew I wasn't safe, but the *thing* in my flat... I knew I couldn't go back. What was it? Would it follow me here? I was in a panic. Should have gone to that A.R.P. officer for help. Too late now. Besides, I wanted to be near Ronny. My heart was racing, and I felt as if I had sick in my throat. I had no mum, no brother, no home, but Ronny would keep me warm and frighten away the *thing*. And if a bomb fell on us, I wouldn't mind so much if we were together.

Impossible though. I couldn't get into the zoo. I was close to Ronny here, but more alone than I had ever been.

Suddenly, there was a violent, deafening bang, and a bright light silhouetted the trees in front of me. A strong wind filled with little stones stung my face and I fell, curled up, covered my eyes until the stones stopped coming. When at last I looked up again, I saw the black trees burning. Millions of sparks were roaring up into the sky. They looked pretty, like fireworks. Bombs were falling all around. Every time the noise went away I realised I was screaming. My mind was empty.

Something huge was coming towards me. I saw its eyes sparkling in the fire's glow. I got up slowly. I saw its big round back, as high as my shoulders. I saw its long thin legs, and sticky up ears. A horse? I saw light and dark stripes. A zebra! It wasn't running, it was walking along as if it didn't mind the bombing. It was just having a nice walk in the park. I felt its warm breath as it came past me, looking at me all the time. And then there was another animal behind it. A donkey! And there was a little foal beside it. They were looking around, trotting to catch up with the zebra. They went past me and they disappeared in the dark. I wasn't screaming now. I didn't even feel scared now. They seemed to know it would all be alright.

I had almost forgotten where I was. But then I thought how strange it was that the animals were walking through the park. How had they got out of the zoo?

And if they had got out, maybe I could get in...

I ran to where they had come from, following the zoo's outside wall. The burning tree made it quite easy to see. There seemed to be more fire actually inside the zoo. I could see the orange smoke and the sparks all going up into the sky, like a volcano, behind the trees and zoo buildings. I kept running towards the fire.

Then I saw the hole in the wall. There were countless bricks and chunks of the wall lying scattered across the grass, and two trees had fallen over. They were in flames too. The whole place was littered with glass and metal and broken wood. I climbed over it all, through the hole, coughing in the smoke and dust. There was another terrifying crack and a huge roar which made everything shake. A bomb had landed very close by. I felt as if I was in a nightmare. I could hear some animals snorting and stamping around me in the darkness. I could smell them too. I was inside the Zebra House. At least there was no fire in here, and they didn't sound hurt, just frightened. I hurried past

the animal enclosures and pushed open the door
that lead out into the zoo. It was dark, but a bright
fire was burning somewhere near the front
entrance. I was in the northernmost part of the zoo
here, and the Lion House was in the southern part,
so I ran past the Giraffe and Hippo House, the
Gazelle Shed, down towards the tunnel under the
road. It was blocked with a wall of sandbags, and
there was a big metal door. It wasn't locked so I
pulled it open. The tunnel was even darker than
the Zebra House, but I ran through it, trailing my
hand along the wall to guide me. My footsteps
echoed all around. I nearly crashed into the
sandbag-wall at the other end, but I put my hands
out to stop me. I heard the horrible screaming and
booming of the bombs as I hurried up the slope and
onto Broad Walk. The explosions made my ribs
shake. All around me, the sky was orange and red.
Little bits of dust and ash were falling on me. I ran
to the Lion House. There were no fires here, but it
was too dark to see if the building was damaged. In
the outside enclosures the lions and jaguars were
walking round and round. The bombs must have
woken them up.

Mr Florey always kept a spare key in the
flowers which hung beside the keeper's entrance. I

found it by feeling. Then I undid the padlock and dropped it on the floor. I heard a bomb whistling down towards me. It seemed to be heading right for me. I heard it smack into the ground somewhere, but there wasn't an explosion. But then another one suddenly landed really close. It felt as if the ground was being shaken like a rug, and I was flat on my face. My ears rang and I felt dizzy. Stones and mud showered down on me. I don't know how long I lay there, but when I sat up, there was a huge cloud of thick smoke right in the middle of Broad Walk. I didn't know what it was at first. It almost looked solid. But it moved like a tree in the wind, and then I saw someone coming through it, staggering. I waited, hoping it was Mr Florey. The smoke cloud swirled and began to drift away.

It wasn't Mr Florey. This person was bent, like an old man, and I could see it had no hair on one side of its head...

The *thing* was there, coming up Broad Walk. It was holding a lantern, and I could see its horrible face. It scraped one of its feet on the floor as it tried to run towards me. I went icy cold. I jumped up, threw open the door and ran down the service corridor. "Ronny!" I called. "It's me! It's Jill!" As I opened the door to his enclosure, I suddenly remembered what Mr Florey had said. Ronny was getting bigger. He wouldn't want me close to him anymore. He could hurt me...

Ronny would never hurt me. I went inside, but I couldn't see anything. It was pitch black. "Ronny!" I whispered. I heard him moving. I heard his deep voice. It wasn't a growl. It was a hello. His huge paws hit my chest and knocked the air out of me. I fell down, and then Ronny was licking my face. His little growl was saying sorry now. I hugged him. His body was huge. His skin was all loose round his ribs, as if he hadn't properly grown into it yet, and his fur was soft. Another bomb fell nearby. I almost wished Ronny and I could die together right now, so we could be with Pete and Mum. Or maybe a bomb would fall on the *thing*, and make it go away. I rubbed Ronny all over and he rolled on his back. I couldn't see him, but it didn't matter.

And then I heard it. The scraping foot. The horrible breathing like a strong wind in the chimney. Suddenly I was more scared of it than of the bombs. I wished I had shut the outside door. I could have locked it from the inside. I was so stupid! Even with Ronny beside me, I was shaking with fear. I couldn't see, but I could hear the *thing* getting closer. Maybe it wouldn't find us in here.

But it stopped right outside the door! And I heard the door squeak open...

I heard that strange, hissing sound as it tried to speak. It coughed, and tried again.

"Jill, Sugar?" came its rasping wheeze. And suddenly in my mind I could see Pete standing there, just like he used to be, in his blue overalls and high boots, leaning on a broom, smiling at me. The lantern's light came into the sleeping compartment. Ronny was lying on his side, but he'd lifted his head up to look at the door. The monster looked in. It had no hair on one side of its head, and its skin was red and blotchy in some places, and scabby and peeling in others. And in some places it looked papery and wrinkled, and was shiny. One side of its nose was all shrivelled, and the nostril was like a small slit. But the eyes were Pete's.

I didn't understand. I felt dizzy with fear and confusion. What *was* it?

"It's me, Sugar. It's Pete. I know I don't look quite like you remember me." Then he started to cough, and he stumbled against the wall. I jumped up.

"Pete?" I said. I still didn't understand.

"It's me, darling. Don't be scared."

And I realised it was fire that had done this to him. But it really was Pete. He had come back!

I hugged him and, at first, he flinched and gently moved my arm: not all his wounds had finished healing. But he managed to hug me back, with one arm, because the other was holding the lantern. He sounded as if he was laughing, but it kept turning into a cough that sounded painful and lasted for ages. I felt his body shaking. It seemed as if he was leaning on me and I was holding him up.

"Oh Jill, Sugar," he said when he stopped coughing. He hung the lantern from a hook in the ceiling. Ronny was standing in front of him now, too. Then, Ronny put one front paw up onto Pete's arm, as if he knew Pete was too weak for him to jump up at. Pete knelt and Ronny licked his face. Pete put his arms round Ronny's neck. I hugged them both. The bombs were still falling all around us, but I had almost forgotten about them.

I suddenly opened my mouth to ask about Mum. Surely, Pete would know where she was. But my fear of the answer made the question stick in my throat. I couldn't make myself say it. I didn't want the horrible truth to spoil this happiness.

And another nasty thought was growing in my

mind. What if Pete wasn't real? What if this was a phantom of Pete? After all, he had appeared from nowhere, like a ghost. What if he had just come back to see me one last time, maybe to save me from the bombs, and then would be gone again, forever?

I realised I was sobbing. I wanted Mum to be with us, holding us, sheltering from the bombs with us. Pete's breathing sounded painful and I could feel him shaking. I thought it must be because he was cold, but he was squeezing my hand so hard he was hurting me. He was making quiet moaning sounds too. He wasn't cold. He was terrified. Clearly, something unimaginably awful had happened to him. I wanted never to let go of him. I wanted him to know I would look after him now, like he had looked after me all my life. And I was afraid if I let go of him he might vanish like a dream.

Chapter 18

The air-raid ended quite suddenly. It was quiet for a while, and then the siren sounded to tell us it was over. I heard bells from the fire engines and ambulances, and people shouting things in the distance. We had survived, and when I had to let go of Pete at last, he didn't vanish. But still, I couldn't force myself to ask him about Mum. Just the thought of what the answer might be made my throat and stomach feel full of ice.

It was as if this wasn't really happening, but I remembered what I still had to do.

"Pete," I said. He didn't answer at first so I said it again.

"Yes, Sugar," he said. He sounded shaky, so I held his hand.

"We've got to save Ronny."

"Save him?"

"They're going to..." I couldn't say it in front of Ronny, of course. I took Pete out into the corridor. "They're going to kill him, like they did to Ronny the First."

"Kill him? Why? How d'you know?" Pete's voice was little more than a thin, rasping whisper.

"He's ill. I saw him being sick. And the new junior keeper told me. We've got to get him out of here."

"We can't do that, Sugar. You can't take a *tiger* out of the *zoo*!"

"We can!" I said, and I had a plan too. "The hole in the wall by the Zebra House. We can get him out there!"

"Blimey, you're serious aren't you."

"'Course I am. We can't let him die. If he's sick, we'll find the money to buy his medicine."

"Where? How? What money?"

"People have been adopting animals in the zoo. We just need to keep asking and asking all over London if we have to. Someone will help." Pete was still shaking his head though. "They're going to kill him if we leave him here, Pete," I said, squeezing his hand, "Just like Ronny the First. K.B.O. remember? Is that what you want?"

"Well..." I could see Pete was thinking about it. "Where would we keep him?"

"We'll find somewhere. Come on, there's no time."

"No, Jill..."

"Well I'm going to do it then. Even if you don't help me." I went back into Ronny's enclosure.

"Come on, Ronny," I said. I couldn't see him, but I heard him get up. He made a growling noise in his throat that made him sound much more dangerous than he really was. He jumped up at me, knocking me flat against the wall. "Not now, Ronny," I said. I pulled the door wide open and he came with me into the corridor. He looked around as if he was a bit nervous. He sniffed the wall, and then he sprayed it from his back end. "Ronny!" I said. "You can't do that here!" I decided I would come back and clean it up later. I had no time now.

"You can't take him out of here," Pete said. His voice went all gurgly and raspy. He started coughing then, but managed to make it stop. Ronny jumped up and put his two front paws on Pete's back, and opened his mouth as if he wanted to chew Pete's head. I knew he wouldn't though. Pete pushed him off. He rubbed Ronny's neck and said, "It's alright, boy." Poor Pete. I could hear his lungs straining at the air, and, as he bent over, hands on knees like an exhausted runner, I realised how weak he was. "I'm sick of all the killing," he breathed quietly. "Maybe... Maybe we *can* save him." Then, he looked around. He took a long piece of rope down from a nail on the wall, and made it into a loop. He tied one end round his own wrist, and I helped him pull it tight. Ronny walked up and down the corridor while we did it, and sprayed the wall a few more times.

"You can't put it round his neck, though," I said. "He won't have that."

"He'll have to, Sugar," Pete said, every word sounding like an effort for him. "You can't let a tiger loose out there. He knows us, and he won't hurt us. But if he gets scared, we don't know what he might do to someone else." I couldn't imagine Ronny hurting anyone, but that is why tigers are kept behind bars, so I had to agree. Pete made a loop in the other end of the rope and tried to put it over Ronny's head. Ronny backed away and growled. "Come on, Ronny," I said, and stroked him behind his ears. Pete tried again, and I kept Ronny looking into my eyes. Pete got the rope over Ronny's neck, but he didn't like it. He pulled away and growled. I'd never heard him growl so loud. It was nearly a roar. He tried to get the rope off with his paws. I hugged him and tried to soothe him. I whispered to him, "It's alright, it's alright." He calmed down a bit, but he still kept shaking his head and growling.

"Come on," Pete said. "I've thought of a place we can take him." He took a couple of deep, wheezing breaths before he could carry on. "There's on old boatshed by the canal that's not used anymore. He'll have to be tied up just in case, but he'll be alright there for now." Ronny pulled on the rope and Pete nearly fell over. "Come on, Ron, it's for your own good," he said.

We went outside. The low part of the sky was orange and red. It looked like sunrise, but it was still the middle of the night. There was the smell of smoke, and the noise of people shouting, and sirens, and fires crackling. Police, or air-raid wardens, were blowing their whistles too. There was a big rumble that made us all jump. I felt the ground shake, like when the bombs exploded. I think it was a building collapsing.

Ronny really didn't like the rope round his neck, and he wouldn't stop pulling, and pawing at it, even when I hugged him and told him to be calm. Somehow, we managed to get him to come with us along Broad Walk. We could see a huge fire out in the park, behind a row of trees. There were other fires in the zoo too, mostly around the North Entrance. I wanted to go and make sure the animals were alright, but I had to get Ronny out first.

There was a wide hole in the ground, right

across Broad Walk. We carefully made our way round it, over all the loose rocks and cobbles and lumps of soil the bomb had made. Ronny stayed close to Pete and I, looking at everything, sniffing and growling. Pete had to pull him hard to get him to go into the dark tunnel, and I hugged his neck and told him it would be alright. Eventually he came with us.

Once out on the other side, we passed the Giraffe and Hippo House with Ronny stopping to sniff everything, and sometimes running ahead, almost pulling Pete over. The Zebra House was just in front of us now, and it must be only a short way to the canal, and the boatshed Pete had in mind. Ronny would be safe soon.

But as we turned up the narrow path between the paddocks, the Zebra House door opened, and a policeman came out. He saw us straight away. He looked at Ronny, and said something which I didn't catch. He stopped and pulled his truncheon out of his belt. He held it in front of him like a sword.

"What's going on?" he said. "Is that a tiger?"

I looked up at Pete. Then the policeman got his silver whistle out of his pocket and blew it three or four times. The high pitched noise made Ronny excited. He seemed to forget about the rope. He started bounding over to the policeman, and Pete couldn't stop him. He nearly fell over again, and he tried to shout, "Ronny! No!" but his voice came out as an exhausted hiss. I shouted too, but Ronny didn't listen. The policeman gave a loud cry, but didn't run away. Two more policeman came through the door now. They stopped when they saw Ronny. Ronny stopped too, and Pete, coughing again, pulled on the rope to make him come away, but Ronny was too strong. The policeman with the truncheon pointed it straight at Ronny's face. The other two looked at each other, and then ran back into the Zebra House.

Then I heard the sound of an engine nearby. There was shouting too, over near where the big fire was. The engine noise came closer.

"Come on, Pete," I shouted. I knew the policeman couldn't stop us. We could just go right past him. The others in the Zebra House had probably run away. But Ronny grabbed the policeman's truncheon and pulled it right out of his hand. The man cried out, but didn't move. I pulled on the rope now, so did Pete, but Ronny wouldn't come. He climbed his front paws onto the policeman's shoulders and rubbed his face all over the man's head, knocking his helmet off.

Behind us, right at the end of the pathway, the zoo lorry stopped.

They must have come to check if any of the animals had escaped. A man jumped out. I heard him say, "Bloody hell, it's a tiger!" and he grabbed his gun from the back of the lorry.

The policeman had fallen to the ground under Ronny. I knew how it looked. Ronny was standing over him as if he was about to eat him.

Then he roared.

It was a proper, grown up tiger roar, like Ronny the First used to do.

"Move!" the man with the gun shouted at me.

"No!" I said. "You can't kill him!"

Pete moved close to me too. He was coughing and struggling to breathe.

"Someone get them out of the way!" the gunman said angrily.

"Good God!" another man cried. "Just kill it!"

There were more people there now. Men and women, around the lorry. I didn't even see where they came from. Some were in their pyjamas and dressing gowns. A lady A.R.P. officer came out of the Zebra House now. We were trapped. She came towards me, smiling, and saying, "It's alright dear. We won't hurt you. You're not in trouble."

It seemed to be snowing, but really it was ash falling from the sky.

The gunman moved so he could shoot past us, but Pete and I moved too, to shield Ronny. "He's friendly!" I called out. "He's not hurting him! Look!" Some of the men had shovels and axes and were slowly coming up the pathway towards us. Ronny had turned away from the policeman to look at them all. The policeman still had his arms across his face, but when Ronny stepped heavily off him, the policeman cautiously got to his feet, then ran past the A.R.P. lady, back into the Zebra House. "Come on you two," one of the men said, but he didn't come too close because of Ronny.

"Let him go!" I cried. "He won't hurt anyone!" I was trying to stay between the gun man and Ronny. So was Pete, but his coughing was getting bad. I think the smoke and ash was making it worse. Just then, Ronny went towards the men, pulling on his rope. Pete almost fell over. The men stopped and backed away. "No, Ronny," I shouted. I knew he wouldn't hurt them, but I didn't want them to think he was going to. I pulled on his rope, and he turned and tried to bite it. The gunman moved and pointed his gun right at Ronny, but I let go of the rope and got in his way again.

"Good God, man," someone said, "Don't hit the girl!"

That was when I realised Pete was on the ground. He was clutching his chest. Ronny stopped biting the rope. He turned and looked at Pete. Then he bounded over to him like a cat pouncing on a cotton reel. He was confused, didn't know if Pete was playing or not. His huge tail swished through the air. He put his big paws either side of Pete, made that deep growling noise in his throat, and licked Pete's head.

And the gunman fired.

Chapter 19

The noise made my heart stop.

Everything went silent. Ronny looked up, and turned his big head. I saw the flames shining in his eyes. I felt as if time had stopped. I waited for him to fall down and die.

But he didn't.

Turning to the gunman, I saw that the gun was angled upwards into the air. Smoke was drifting from it. Mr Florey, who I hadn't even realised was there, was still holding the man's arm. He must have pushed it up, just in time. "Put this damn thing away," Mr Florey said, "before you kill someone." He was in pyjamas and dressing gown, and had his Wellington boots on. "Put those weapons down, men. You ought to know better. And get a doctor. The lad needs some help!"

I ran over to Pete. His face was bright red, and there was saliva hanging from his lips. He wasn't coughing any more, but I could hear his breaths whistling. Ronny sat down next to us, and looked around at all the people. Mr Florey came over, too. He didn't have his spectacles on, and his hair was sticking up all over the place.

"My God, Pete," he said. He recognised him instantly, just like Ronny had done. I felt ashamed of myself then. "You've been through it lad, eh?" Pete nodded, but didn't manage to smile. "Don't try to speak," Mr Florey said. "You just relax now. Everything'll be alright. There'll be a doctor here soon." He took off his dressing gown and wrapped it round Pete's shoulders. Ronny licked Mr Florey's head, and made his hair stand up even more. Other people were getting closer now, but they all still looked scared. Ronny looked up at them, and some of them jumped and backed away. He stood there, close by me, watching everyone. He seemed calmer now.

"What the devil were you thinking, Jill?" Mr Florey said, softly.

"They're going to kill him, aren't they?" I whispered, so Ronny wouldn't hear.

"What, these people? No."

"I mean Doctor Barker, and the zoo people. That's why I was rescuing him."

"No, no they're not."

"They are. The man told me; the new junior keeper. He said Ronny won't be around for long. He's sick."

"He said he's sick?"

"No, but I saw Ronny being sick."

A man came over to Pete, slowly, watching Ronny. I recognised him from the zoo. The man in the suit who had been in charge of killing all the animals when the war started, including Ronny the First. He was wearing a brown, patterned jumper and grey trousers this time. He had his bowler hat on, though. He offered Pete a drink from a flask. I could smell coffee as Pete sipped it. Mr Florey told him to look after Pete. Then he told another young man to go and fetch Ronny a joint of meat from the Lion House refrigerator. "We'd better get Ronny back where he belongs," he said to me. We got up, and Ronny stood too, watching everyone. Mr Florey untied the rope from Pete's wrist. "It's alright," he announced to the people close by, "I've got 'im tight." Ronny didn't want to leave Pete, but the smell of the meat the young man returned with made him start licking his lips.

I gave Pete a hug and kissed him. He felt cold and sweaty. He managed to smile, but he could barely even look up. I had to leave him though. I had to help get Ronny back.

***

A little while later, Ronny was back in his cage. It had been hard work. Ronny was really strong and had pulled a lot on his rope. Mr Florey and I were exhausted, so we were sitting on the wooden benches at the back of the public viewing hall, watching him for a minute, before going back to find Pete. Because of the blackout, the other young man had put some candles on the floor instead of switching on the electric lights. Then he'd gone to help put out the fires, and check for escaped animals. Before he went, I remembered to tell him about the zebra and the donkey I'd seen in the park.

I could hardly see Ronny, but his eyes were like sparks in the darkness.

"Now then, tell me again why you tried to... *rescue* him," Mr Florey said.

"He's sick, isn't he?" I said. "I saw him."

"He's still prone to bouts of sickness, yes," Mr Florey explained. "His immunities are weak. Probably always will be. He's been close to death before, yes, but it's nothing too serious at the moment. There're no plans to have him K.B.O." He looked at me for a while. I think he was deciding what to tell me. He sighed. "You're a tough lass, Jilly. Sometimes the truth can be hard to handle, but I reckon you're up to the task. I wish I could tell you Ronny will live forever. Or even for as long as a tiger should. But I can't. That is the sad truth. But right now, with good medication, and you as his friend, his future is bright. I suppose the only thing you have to decide is..."

He paused, so I finished his sentence for him.

"...Whether I would rather have him as a friend even though he is sick, or not have him at all." Pete's advice made sense to me now, and I had already made my decision.

Mr Florey laughed. "You never stop surprising me, young lady," he said. "Now I'm going to tell you the good bit." Ronny was looking up at us from his cage, as if he was excited to hear the good bit too. "Just like the lad told you, Ronny won't be around for long. Well, not round here anyway. Do you remember that strange fellow, Mr Kendal? You know, the wolf-man?" I nodded. "Of course you do," Mr Florey said, smiling. "Well, you may just have done more good than you could ever have imagined when you wrote him that letter. He's agreed to take care of Ronny down in Kent, at his house. He has a sizable menagerie there, you know. It seems you made quite an impression on him. He always asks about you. He was delighted by your letter.

He read it right in front of me. You know, I have to admire your creativity. Your corned beef tin label may have saved Ronny's life!" My mouth was wide open. I didn't dare let myself feel happy yet in case this wasn't really happening. "He's always wanted a tiger, but they're not easy to come by, and it looks as if that's the only way he's going to get one." Mr Florey had a handkerchief in his hand now, and he wiped my face. I didn't even know I was crying. "What's more, I think he'd like some help looking after Ronny. Don't you?"

I nodded. I wasn't sure what he meant though.

"It's all been arranged, dear. Your mum seems to have struck up quite the friendship with Mr Kendal. He's been up to London a few times since—"

"My mum?" I *had* to ask about her now. "Where is she? Do you know where she is?"

"Well, I believe she's gone to Belford, to bring you back. Somehow, you seem to have missed each other."

"So... she's alive then?"

"Alive and frantically worried about you, I should imagine. Poor woman. She's probably going through hell as we speak. I expect she'll be on the first train back here again tomorrow."

I couldn't stop myself smiling. I cried with happiness and hugged Mr Florey.

A few minutes later, someone came and told us Pete had been taken to hospital. My new happiness suddenly disappeared and I felt sick again. Mr Florey drove me there in his car. It seemed ages before we found him. It was an awful place to be. There were lots of people who had been injured in the air-raids. People were crying and moaning in pain. Some were calling out for the doctors, and the corridors were full. I felt terrible for them, but I couldn't help them. Some were walking about, some were on beds. Some people were running around looking for members of their family, and everywhere there was the strong smell of disinfectant. Mr Florey, who was still wearing his pyjamas, was really calm. He kept telling me Pete would be fine now he was being looked after. He asked a nurse for help, and eventually found out where Pete was.

Pete had a mask over his face connected to a big tank of gas standing beside his bed. I hated seeing him looking so ill. But he was awake, and he managed to smile at me. He held my hand, and I saw how badly burnt his was. It was covered in lumpy, shiny scars. I couldn't stop crying, with happiness for having Pete back alive, and with sorrow for what had happened to him. The nurses said he had a bad chest infection, and his lungs had been damaged by whatever fire had burned him so badly. He needed lots of rest.

Mr Florey took me home to his house. His wife was really kind. It was almost daylight, but she said I needed to sleep. Their spare room was so warm and cosy, once Mr Florey had lit the fire. The blackout curtains were closed, and for the first time in ages, I didn't feel scared of the dark. In fact, as soon as I curled up between the cool, soft sheets, I fell fast asleep. In the afternoon, Mrs Florey cooked us eggs and bacon. The smell of it woke me up. It was delicious, and I wolfed it down ravenously. I said, "Thank you," and she said, "You are so welcome, young lady." I said, "I am sorry I ate so much," and she said, "Oh, get away!"

Then Mr Florey and I went back to the hospital. Pete was looking better. He was allowed to have the mask off for a while. Somehow, his face didn't look so badly burnt today. Maybe I was just getting used to it, but I thought he looked a bit more like the old Pete.

Mr Florey left us alone for a while. Pete told me he had come back to London just a few days ago.

He didn't tell me how he had got so badly hurt. I asked him but he just looked away. I think he was badly hurt on the inside too. But later I found out he'd been left behind by the army in Norway after a bomb had exploded near to him, and made a burning building collapse. Everyone must have thought he was dead. All he knew was he woke up in a bed in the attic of a large house, being looked after by a young woman and her grandma. They looked after him for weeks, months even, and he didn't even speak their language. As soon as his wounds had healed enough, and he could walk again, they had helped him get to Sweden, which was neutral, meaning it wasn't really taking part in the war. After that, he'd spent weeks in danger and hardship, making his way back to England.

He told me that Mum had written to me to tell me all the news, and to ask how I would feel about us all going to stay with Mr Kendal until the war was over. But when she read my letter about Mrs Hill she realised I hadn't received hers. She decided not to write back again, in case Mrs Hill read it and got even nastier. Instead, she decided just to go to Belford, to give Mrs Hill a piece of her mind, and to fetch me back herself. But that was the day I ran away.

Pete had stayed at home when Mum went to Belford, but had managed a walk in the park, and a meeting with some friends. The doctor had told him it was important to keep exercising his limbs, to keep his burned skin supple, and to breathe fresh air into his injured lungs. He hadn't realised I was in the flat, asleep in bed, when he came home.

Pete knew all about Mr Kendal too. He seemed to have taken a shine to my mum, and Mum had taken one to him. I felt a bit funny when I heard that. I didn't know why. But Mr Kendal had talked to Doctor Barker, and arranged to take care of Ronny in his menagerie. He wasn't actually buying him, but he was fostering him until the war was over.

It was during my afternoon hospital visit that I saw Pete looking at something behind me. I turned round to see what it was.

Mum was coming towards us.

I put my hand over my mouth to stop myself shouting out, and before I knew it she had her arms tight around me.

Chapter 20

Mr Kendal's house wasn't a big country house like I'd expected. It was a lot bigger than our flat in London though. It was an ordinary-looking, red brick house on the corner of two main roads in a town in Kent. It had ivy growing on the walls. Mr Kendal had two spare bedrooms. Mum and I slept in one, and Pete would have the other one when he came out of hospital.

I couldn't wait to have him back.

Mr Kendal's house had a huge garden all around it and that was where he kept all his animals. There were lots of large enclosures made of wood and metal and wire, and I could not believe all the animals he had. There were three wolves and a lion, a jaguar and some monkeys and a dingo, which is a big, scruffy-looking, wild dog. There was even an aviary. At first, I could hardly speak, I was so amazed and excited. Then I started asking questions about the animals, and Mr Kendal always had the answers.

And there was one enclosure with nothing in it yet. That was for Ronny.

He arrived a few days after us. Mr Florey

brought him down. Mr Kendal and I had spent the whole morning in the front garden, leaning on the wall, waiting. I decided I did like him. His long moustache looked like a small, yellow bird with its wings spread, and in a way, I felt that suited him. And he had friendly eyes. He didn't smile with his mouth, but he smiled with his eyes, so that they twinkled. He had a soft voice, and he talked to me all about his animals. I think I liked him so much because I could tell he loved his animals. And I think he liked me because I did too. He always called me Jilly, and he said I could call him Fred, if I liked.

And when we saw the lorry I shouted, "Mum! Mum! He's here!"

Mum came hurrying out of the house, drying her hands on a tea towel. Of course, I wanted Pete to be there. It felt wrong for him to miss this, but I knew he'd be back with us soon.

Ronny's cage was covered up with a big green tarpaulin. That was so he didn't scare people on the journey down. When Mr Florey and Fred jumped on the back of the lorry and lifted one side of the tarpaulin, I saw Ronny lying down on the straw. He looked as if he'd been asleep. Mum was beside me now, with her arm round my shoulders. I held her hand, and I imagined Dad was with us too. I remembered my dream, when he'd told me I could save Ronny if I really tried. I wished I could thank him, but somehow I felt he knew that. I also had to thank Tim. In fact, he might even have received my letter by now. Mrs Hill would have received the money, too. Mum had made me write to Mrs Hill, apologising for taking it, and for running away, even though she agreed Mrs Hill had left me with no choice. I hoped Mary would read the letter too, but Mum had said I wasn't to mention the money of mine which had gone missing, which meant I couldn't explain why I'd stolen from them. I *sort of* understood why not. Mum said I shouldn't make excuses for my actions, even if there were perfectly good excuses to make. Anyway, at least it meant Mrs Hill might let Tim come and visit us some time.

Ronny looked at us all, and made that deep rumbling noise in his throat. That was his way of saying hello.

Author's Note

Even though this novel is a work of fiction, much of what happens in it is based on historical fact. For instance, when the war began, some dangerous animals were K.B.O. (You know by now what that means!) Well, you couldn't have poisonous snakes escaping in an air-raid, and slithering about all over London, could you? And because of shortages in medicines and some foods, other animals were more at risk too. Despite what Jill thought, this was not cruelty. It was a tragic necessity. I don't suppose that anyone working at the zoo liked that fact.

Just like all the other characters in the book, including Ronny himself, Dr Barker never existed. However, if he did, I think you'd find he was a tough, stern man, but a man with a good heart underneath it all. He was a vet, and as such he would have loved all the zoo's animals. But his job had a very difficult, very sad side too, and he had to take that in his stride. I'm sure Jill would have understood that, eventually.

Some other elements of the story are true. During the war, a number of bombs did fall in the zoo, though very little damage was done. A zebra and a donkey (or rather, an ass) escaped, but were quickly rounded up and safely returned. A number of monkeys escaped and ran wild for several days too! A lot of the animals were evacuated to Whipsnade, where they would have been much safer. You'll no doubt be pleased to learn that no animals in London Zoo were killed or even seriously injured by bombs throughout the entire war, despite the damage done to some of the buildings they were in.

Jill had an awful time as an evacuee, and some of the things that happened to her – sleeping under the table, eating everyone else's leftovers, having to do endless chores – are based on firsthand accounts from real-life evacuees. However, I think that many evacuees were treated well, and some thoroughly enjoyed the whole experience.